Catherine Cookson was born in East Jarrow and the place of her birth provides the background she so vividly creates in many of her novels. Although acclaimed as a regional writer – her novel THE ROUND TOWER won the Winifred Holtby Award for the best regional novel of 1968 – her readership spreads throughout the world. Her work has been translated into twelve languages and Corgi alone has over 27,000,000 copies of her novels in print, including those written under the name of Catherine Marchant.

Mrs Cookson was born the illegitimate daughter of a poverty-stricken woman, Kate, whom she believed to be her older sister. Catherine began work in service but eventually moved south to Hastings where she met and married a local grammar school master. At the age of forty she began writing with great success about the lives of the working class people of the North-East with whom she had grown up, including her intriguing autobiography, OUR KATE. Her many bestselling novels have established her as one of the most popular contemporary women novelists.

Mrs Cookson now lives in Northumberland.

and published by Corgi Books

Catherine Cookson

Marriage and
Mary Ann

CORGI BOOKS

MARRIAGE AND MARY ANN

A CORGI BOOK 0 552 09076 X

First published in Great Britain by
Macdonald & Co. (Publishers) Ltd.

PRINTING HISTORY
Macdonald edition published 1964
Macdonald edition reprinted 1967
Corgi edition published 1972
Corgi edition reprinted 1973
Corgi edition reprinted 1974
Corgi edition reprinted 1976
Corgi edition reprinted 1977
Corgi edition reprinted 1978
Corgi edition reprinted 1979
Corgi edition reprinted 1980 (twice)
Corgi edition reprinted 1982
Corgi edition reprinted 1984

This book is set in 10-10½ pt. Intertype Baskerville

Corgi Books are published by
Transworld Publishers Ltd.,
Century House, 61–63 Uxbridge Road,
Ealing, London W5 5SA

Set, printed and bound in Great Britain by
Cox & Wyman Ltd., Reading, Berks.

Marriage and
Mary Ann

CHAPTER ONE

'AND all this has come about because they went on a holiday.' Fanny McBride thrust out her thick arm and pulled the blue sugar bag towards her, and after ladling three spoonfuls into an outsize cup of tea she added, 'But you're sure you're not enlargin' on everything, Mary Ann?'

'No, Mrs. McBride. I wish I was. But it isn't imagination, it isn't.'

'Well, I was just thinkin' you have a lot on your mind at the present moment, with Michael and Sarah's wedding in the offing, and your own looming up ahead. By the way, I must tell you, I was glad when you and Corny decided not to make it a double-do. I think you want your own glory on a day like that.' Fanny smiled broadly at Mary Ann. 'Aw' – she shook her head – 'the day I see you and Corny married I think my heart'll burst for joy. I've known you since you were that high' – she measured a short distance with her hand – 'and I've watched you grow up to great things.'

'Aw, Mrs. McBride.' Mary Ann was shaking her head as she stared down towards the table. 'I've done nothing with me life, nothing as yet.'

'Not for yourself you haven't, me dear, except to take me grandson for your husband, but you've done it for others. Where would your da be the day without you and your schemes, eh?' She poked her broad face towards that of the heart-shaped, elfin face of Mary Ann. 'Would Mike be managing a farm with a grand house, an' be the right hand of Mr. Lord, if it be his only hand?'

'It was through me he lost his hand, don't forget that, Mrs. McBride.'

'Do I forget that God works in strange ways, child? If Mike hadn't lost his hand he wouldn't be where he is the day.'

'I know that.'

'Well then, you've no need to bother your head about the things you haven't done, for to my mind you've achieved almost the impossible where your da's concerned. As you know, I'm very fond of Mike, an' I know him inside out, his strength and his one weakness, an' that being the drink. But he's conquered that, thanks be to God. Well, knowing him as I do, I wouldn't have said that he had a weakness for the women, although I could say that some women might have a weakness for himself, for the older he gets the more fetchin' he gets.'

'That's the trouble.'

Mary Ann was looking solemnly at this big, voluptuous old woman, who, as she had said, had known her from a small child. And from a small child Mary Ann had looked upon Fanny McBride as her friend and comforter. From the day they had first come to live in the attic of Mulhattan's Hall – which place her mother had considered the very end of the downward trail – from that day she had been comforted and helped by the tenant on the first floor, Mrs. Fanny McBride. There was no one else in the world she could talk to freely about her da, except to this woman, because, as Fanny had also stated, she knew Mike Shaughnessy inside out.

Mary Ann said now, 'It seems sad to think that it was my mother's first real holiday, and she had been looking forward to it so much; and we all had fun and carry-on before they went saying what would happen to them at a holiday camp. The awful thing is that it was herself who plumped to go to a holiday camp; me da wasn't for it at all, he just went to please her.'

'How old did you say the girl was?'

'Nineteen.'

'And she has red hair?'

'Yes, and my mother says that's how it started. They were at the same table and her mother – the girl's mother, Mrs. Radley – pointed out that me da's hair was almost the same shade as her daughter's. Then he danced with her, and after that they were in the swimming pool together. My mother can't swim and she just had to sit and look on. At first she didn't think anything about it, until Mrs. Radley and her –

Yvonne, they call her – tacked on to them everywhere they went . . . and me da seemed to like it.'

'And your mother told you all this?'

'Yes.'

Fanny shook her head again. 'Lizzie must be upset in her mind to speak of it so plainly, because she was ever so close about some things was Lizzie, reserved like, about the private things in her life, even when she was upstairs here. She must be taking this very badly, and it's hitting her at the wrong time of life. But then, that always happens; these things always hit women at the wrong time of life. I think men were built to cause it to be so, just to make things harder for us.'

'She can't set her mind to the wedding because they're coming.'

'Who was it asked them?'

'It must have been me da because she says that she never did.'

'Well, it needn't have been him, you know, Mary Ann. People, clever people, have a way of gettin' themselves invited – aye! begod, even into me house here.' She laughed. 'They put you on a spot. Perhaps your da was put on a spot; I wouldn't lay that at his door.'

Mary Ann rose from the table and walked to the window, and, looking out through the narrow aperture of the curtains down into the dull, sunless street, she turned her gaze towards the top end from where she hoped to see Corny coming, and then she fingered the curtains before saying, 'He must have known that if she came to the wedding me mother would be upset, and if he didn't ask them outright he could have done something to put them off. That's what's in me mind all the time. I hate to think of him deliberately hurting me mother.'

Fanny, pulling herself to her feet by gripping the worn, wooden arms of her chair, shambled towards the open fire, and there, lifting up the long rake, she pulled some pieces of coal from the back of the grate down into the dulling embers. Then, placing the rake back on the fender, she said, 'Tell me, was he pleased to see them when they came on the hop last Sunday?'

'Yes . . . yes, he was. He seemed a bit taken aback at first, but then he started to act like a young lad, skittish. I . . . oh, Mrs. McBride. . . .' Mary Ann turned from the window and looked across the cluttered, dusty room to the old woman, and she bit on her lip before she ended, 'He made me so ashamed. I . . . I never thought I would feel like that about him . . . ashamed of him. It was . . . it was a different kind of feeling to when he used to get roaring drunk. I wasn't really ashamed of him then, only sorry for him, pitying him, sort of; but last Sunday I . . . I knew I was ashamed of him. Oh . . . oh, Mrs. McBride, it was awful. I . . . I can say this to you, can't I, because I've always been able to talk to you, haven't I?'

'Aye, hinny, you have that,' said Fanny in a low tone. 'It's another thing I've thanked God for. Go on.'

Mary Ann came and took her seat at the table again, and, moving the spoon round in the empty cup, she concentrated her gaze on it as she said, 'Well, there was a time when I began to dislike me mother for certain things she did, for her attitude towards the front room. . . . Remember, when she didn't want Sarah to have it. And then the way she used to go for me da at times. But I could never imagine me ever disliking me da, because you know . . .' She lifted her eyes to those of Mrs. McBride and said very softly, 'I worship him, I really do. At least I did. He was like God to me, but when I saw him actually put his arm round that beastly, scheming cat's waist' – her lips were now squared from her teeth – 'I felt that I hated him.'

'Where did this happen?'

'It was in the kitchen, but me mother was there.'

'Aw well, that's not so bad. It would have meant something much worse if she hadn't been there.'

'I don't see it like that, Mrs. McBride, for if he'll do that in front of her what'll he do when she isn't there? That's how I see it. And . . . and he's started sprucing up. He never used to get changed in the evening unless he was going out, because sometimes he's got to see to the cattle late on, but now after tea he goes upstairs and gets into a good suit, collar and tie and everything.'

'Does he take himself out?'

'One night last week he did.'

'Did you know where he went?'

'No. He didn't say, and me mother didn't ask him, and I wouldn't. But on other nights he just strolled round the fields all dressed up like that.'

Returning to her chair, Fanny lowered herself slowly down, her head wagging the while. She sucked in her lips, closed her eyes, and, joining her hands together, moved these too in a wagging movement; then simultaneously all these actions ceased and she looked straight ahead towards the fire as she said, 'Within a few months you'll be married, Mary Ann, an' life will open out for you, an' you'll learn lots of things. But they all won't come at once, an' let's thank God for it, but it'll be some time afore you come really aware of the fact that there comes a period in life when women are not themselves. You'll have likely heard without under-standing much about it that the middle years are very trying to a woman, but nobody's likely told you, for nobody seems to think along the same lines regarding men, but . . .' Now Fanny swung her head round towards Mary Ann, and, pointing her finger at her, she said solemnly, 'But now, let me tell you, because I know, havin' reared a number of the specimens, that men are tested much more sorely than women during the middle years, maybe not along the same lines, but nevertheless they are tested. There's something stirs in them, aggravatin' them, seeming to say "Come on, lad, you're not dead yet. Show them that you're as young as ever you were." An' there, Mary Ann, you've got the core of the whole matter . . . as young as ever they were. Now a woman doesn't like growin' old, it hurts her vanity; even if she's as ugly as sin it hurts her vanity. But, begod, a man likes growin' old less, for it not only hurts his vanity, it threatens his manhood. He is torn to shreds in that way much more than a woman is. Men, you know, Mary Ann, are merely grown-up lads. They may look old, and act old, but under their skins they're just lads, an', as I've said, there comes a time when they want to prove to the world they're still lads, so what do they do? Well, they take up with a lass young enough to be their daughter, some young enough to be a granddaughter. Now as I see it, this is what's happening to your da, an' your mother should know all about this. There's no doubt she does, but she's troubled in herself, an' in me own opinion Lizzie's no fit person to handle this situation at all. No, as I see it she's not; but you, Mary Ann, you with all your experience of your da, you're the one best able to talk to him.'

'Oh no. Oh no.' Mary Ann was again on her feet. 'I couldn't Mrs. McBride, not about this.'

'But you've done it on other occasions, you've talked him round from other things than drink.'

'Yes, well . . . but I haven't so much talked to him as did things . . . Oh, I can't explain.'

'There's no need to, I know. As I said afore, you've schemed and manoeuvred. . . . Well, why not use the same tactics now?'

'I couldn't, Mrs. McBride; I tell you, I just couldn't, not over this. Him going mad over this girl, this young girl. I've thought about it but I just couldn't. I . . . I can't even speak to him ordinarily.'

'You mean you're not speaking to Mike at all?'

'No, I haven't for the past three weeks.'

'Aw, God in heaven! Now you are askin' for trouble.'

'Well, I can't help it.'

'Well now, Mary Ann' – the fat, not too clean, finger was wagging at her again – 'you'll just have to help it, for that's the worst thing you could do, not be speakin' to him. . . . Tell me, how's Lizzie treatin' him?'

'She hardly speaks to him either.'

'Name of God! I thought you both had more sense, at least you. If you want to drive him away that's the way to do it. Go on not speakin' to him, push him out, and that girl, with the help of her mother, will have him in her arms afore you can say Jimmy McGregor. Now look. . . . Aw' – Fanny turned her head towards the door – 'if I know that step, this is the Lado himself, so we'll take this matter up another time. But think on what I've said.'

Mary Ann, too, was looking towards the door, and when it opened she managed a smile for the young man entering.

Corny Boyle was now six foot two and broad with it. He had a fine physique, and if he'd had a matching face he might have been billed as a modern Apollo, but Corny could lay no claim to good looks. His best feature were his eyes; for the rest, his face gave the impression of a piece of granite that had been hacked by a would-be sculptor. He looked older than his twenty-three years, in fact he could at times have passed for thirty; this was when his face was in repose, for when he smiled he looked youthful. It could be said that to Corny's one good feature you could add his smile, for it was an impish, irresistible smile, and it infected those it fell upon, it even at times gave some people the impression that he was handsome. It had this latter effect on Mary Ann.

'Hello, Gran.' He took three strides across the room to Fanny's side, and, bending over her, he kissed her cheek, while she placed her hand on his thick hair. Then, looking towards Mary Ann, he said, 'Hello, you.'

'Hello yourself. You've been some time. You said four o'clock.'

'I know I did but I'm only half-an-hour out and I knew you'd be here, sitting gossiping' – he glanced towards Fanny – 'and so . . .'

At this point Mary Ann, bouncing her head, took up his words, and together they chanted, 'And so I went and had a look at Meyer's garage.'

Fanny's head was back now and her laugh was filling the room. 'Aw, begod, you're startin' early! Well, as long as he wasn't in Flanagan's bar, or at the bettin' shop waitin' the result of the last race, it isn't too bad, eh?' She put her hand out towards Mary Ann, and Mary Ann, laughing, replied, 'That's all he can talk about, cars, cars, cars.'

'Well, as I'll have to support you on cars for the rest of your life what better subject could I talk about?' Corny bent his long length above her and they stared at each other for a moment, their faces becoming solemn; then, doubling his fist, he twice punched her gently on the side of the chin before saying, 'Well, if you want to go to that dance and go home first, you'll have to get a move on.'

'Oh! A move on! We're now all bustle and hurry.' Mary Ann inclined her head towards Fanny's broadly smiling face, and as Corny exclaimed, 'Who is it wants to go to the dance, anyway?' she put on her coat and hat and, turning to Fanny, said softly, 'Bye-bye, Mrs. McBride, and thanks ... for the tea and everything.'

'Thank you, hinny, for comin' in.'

'Bye-bye, Gran.' Again Corny kissed the networked skin, but before he straightened up he cast his glance towards Mary Ann, saying, 'Don't you think it's time you called this old faggot Gran, instead of Mrs. McBride?'

Fanny and Mary Ann looked at each other, then with a small smile Mary Ann said, 'I suppose so, but somehow ... well, I always think of you as Mrs. McBride and it's got the same feeling as me saying ma, or da. ... You understand?'

'I understand, hinny, an' I'll remain Mrs. McBride. An', you know, I like it that way, it's got a dignified ring, don't you think ... Mrs. McBride?'

'Dignified!' Corny now took the flat of his hand and pushed the big broad face to one side, exclaiming, 'You, dignified! ... You're in your dotage, woman.'

'Get out of it, an' this minute, or I'll let you see who's in their dotage ... or an old faggot at least.'

Fanny pulled herself up and brandished her fist at him, and Corny, pushing Mary Ann into the passage and about to follow her, looked back into the room and said softly, 'Go on with you, fat old Fan. Dignified, indeed!'

Her grandson's words could have been a compliment, for they brought a warm tender smile to Fanny's face, and when the door closed on him she sat down again, and the smile remained with her as she looked about her with eyes that did not take in the muddle and dust amidst which she sat; for what was muddle she would have said if she had thought about it, and what was dust when your heart was happy knowing that your favourite grandson had had the good sense to pick himself the nicest little lass in the world?

In the street, the nicest little lass walked sedately by Corny's side. She always felt slightly self-conscious when with him in the street, for she remembered experiences when children had shouted after them, 'De ya want a step-ladder, miss?' and, 'Aa'll bunk you up to him for thrup-pence.' Then there was the day when the woman behind them in the bus said, 'That's the long an' the short of it, isn't it?' And so she resisted her desire to link arms with him, for in her mind's eye she could see how ludicrous it would look. Even when they held hands it must appear to other people as if he was taking a child for a walk. She was five foot tall and, try as she might, she couldn't add a fraction of an inch to this. Her height wasn't noticeable when she was on her own, only when she was with Corny, for besides being small she was slightly built, and this didn't help matters.

'You're quiet,' he said, 'what's the matter?'

'Nothing.'

'Well, it couldn't be much less, could it?' They turned their eyes towards each other and smiled, and the smiles brought a humorous twist to their faces.

'Want to go to that dance?'

Mary Ann moved one shoulder, 'I'm not really particular, I'd just as soon go to the pictures or the bowling alley. What about you?'

'Anything'll suit me. I tell you what though. . . .' He moved nearer to her and, his voice dropping to a whisper, he went on, 'I've got some new car catalogues. We could have a smashing time just sitting looking at them.'

Forcing herself not to laugh, she pushed at him with her elbow as she replied, 'That would be wonderful. You wouldn't like us to sit on that seat outside Meyer's garage, would you?'

'Aw.' He moved his head as if in wonder. 'Aw, that would be simply marvellous, just to sit all the night looking at Meyer's garage and them cars.'

'You're barmy. Cars, cars, cars.'

Now her tone had an edge to it, and he mimicked it, saying, 'Cars, cars, cars.' Then went on, 'Yes, I'm barmy about them all right, an' before you're finished you'll be glad I'm barmy about them, because cars, cars, cars, are going to get you all you want. . . . In the end they will, anyway.'

'How do you know what I want? For all you know I might want you to go round the streets playing your cornet.'

He slanted his eyes down at her for a moment, then said quietly, 'Look, what's up with you? You're ratty about something. Anything happened in me grannie's?'

17

'Of course not. What could happen in there?'

'Only talk. . . . What were you talking about?'

'Oh, nothing. Look, there's the bus.' She pointed. 'If we miss it, it'll be another half-an-hour.'

Grabbing her arm, he ran with her, almost lifting her off the ground, and he actually hoisted her on to the platform of the bus just as it was about to move away.

Half-an-hour later they were in the country, walking up the lane towards the farm. Although it was a dull day the field to the right of them seemed lit by sunshine, for, with the breeze passing over them, the full heads of barley were making waves of light and shade.

Mary Ann's eyes, following the waves, were lifted into the far distance to the big house on the hill, Mr. Lord's house . . . and now Tony's house . . . and Lettice's house. It was strange to think of Tony married to Lettice and then both living with Mr. Lord . . . and he liking it. Why was it, she asked herself now, that in spite of her good intentions she always felt the slightest bit of jealousy when she thought of Mr. Lord liking Lettice living with him? Although she herself had had a hand in Mr. Lord's acceptance of his grandson's wife, she still couldn't help the feeling that she didn't want him to be too happy about it. . . . But she really knew what caused this feeling. It was the fear that if he became too engrossed in Tony and his wife he would forget all about her.

'You're not listening to me.'

'What? What did you say?'

Pulling her to a stop, Corny placed his hands on her shoulders and surveyed her through narrowed eyes before saying, 'I said, if they make that branch road off the Newcastle road and come up by Meyer's garage, and if we get the garage, we're made. That's what I said. I've been talking since we got off the bus and you haven't heard a word.'

'You're always talking.' She smiled tenderly up at him. 'But you don't talk to the right people.'

'Oh, don't I?' He raised his brows. 'Well, I'll have to find the right people, won't I? But for the present I'll keep practising on you, to get me fit for the real thing. . . . And that's another thing, I was talking about the real thing a minute ago, but you weren't with me. We are going to have a wedding, aren't we?'

'Yes.' She blinked her eyes. The smile was still on her face, but when he snapped his body upwards away from her, exclaiming harshly, 'You're as interested in what I'm saying as if I was talking about a Methodist Sunday School treat,' she cried: 'All right! All right! Don't go on like that.' She swung away, her voice cracking now. 'I might as well tell you I can't think of the wedding . . . so there. I can't think of anything but me da at the present moment.'

'God in Heaven!' Corny put his fist to his brow. 'Don't start on that again – it'll work out. Men go through these phases. . . . It'll work out.'

As she stared at him she thought, That's what Mrs. McBride said. It's a phase and it'll work out. But what if it doesn't work out?

'How do you know it'll work out?' she demanded now. 'Have you been through the phase?'

'I don't happen to be in me forties.' The impatient note in his voice caused her to respond with, 'Oh, it happens in the forties, does it? Then you've got something to look forward to, haven't you?'

'Aye, yes.' He put on a false smile and his tone was harsh now as he went on, 'I hadn't thought about it in that way. You've got a point there. And, by lad, by the time I've lived with you until I'm forty I imagine I'll be damned glad of a little variety . . . that is, if I manage to stick it out that long.'

'Manage-to-stick-it-out-that-long!' She spaced his words. 'Well, I can tell you here and now, Mr. Cornelius Boyle, there'll be no need to endure any purgatory through me.'

They were off again. Their association had always taken this pattern: sunshine, then sudden storm, then sunshine again.

'Good . . . good.' He was towering over her, glaring down at her. 'So we're breaking up. That's it, isn't it?'

'Yes, that's it.'

They stood for a long moment exchanging their momentary animosity, then with a swiftness that startled her his hands were under her oxters and he had lifted her off her feet, and he was kissing her, a hard, rough kiss. Then still holding her to him, he said softly, 'I had to have that for the road, seeing that I'll be on my own for the next forty years.' Now both their bodies began to shake and melt into each other. Her arms were around his neck as she repeated, 'Oh, Corny! Corny! I'm daft I am. I'm daft.'

'I know you are.'

'I mean about me da.'

'That's what I mean an' all; but I tell you he'll get over it.'

'But me mother's worried sick, Corny. And it's the disgrace, and with a young girl. Do you know she's months younger than me?'

'She looks ten years older, and I'm not kiddin'.'

'That's as may be, but she's younger, and when I see her with me da . . . oh, it makes me sick, and I just can't believe it. I can't believe he can be so silly, so nauseatingly silly.'

'Has it happened like this afore?'

They were walking slowly up the lane now, their arms about each other.

'No, not like this, but there have been women who have fallen for him. But then, as I say, they were women, not girls.'

'Did he have affairs with them – I mean the women?'

'No, no, never; he just laughed at them, and laughed about them to me ma. Not that she wasn't worried once or twice, like the time she thought he was gone on Mrs. Quinton.'

'Mrs. Quinton? Bob Quinton's wife? She's a smasher.'

'There you go . . . smasher. Well, perhaps she is a smasher but she liked me da.' She nodded her head up at him. 'But this present business is different; it's – it's nasty, and it's keeping on.'

'It's just because he's flattered. Look, do as I say, let things rest and take their course.'

'I can't, Corny, because I'm frightened, really I am. I know it's as you say, it's because she flatters him. And her mother and all, she's as bad, and he laps it up. . . . All the more so now because me mother doesn't let on he's there. . . Well, you know what I mean? But she hasn't made much of him for a long time, because she hasn't been feeling too good herself.' She stopped in the road and, twisting round, looked up at him, saying, 'Do you know, I can see both their minds working, both that sly cat's and her mother's. They've got it all set between them. I'll be out of the way when I get married; Michael and Sarah will be in the bungalow; so there will be only me mother and me da left, and now that it's open knowledge that the farm will be me da's one day they think they're on to a good thing. Miss Yvonne's just got to have an affair with me da . . . get herself a baby, and then me mother's out. . . .'

'Mary Ann!' As Corny loosened his hold on her he drew his chin into his neck, and the action seemed to pull his voice up from deep down in his chest. 'Don't talk like that,' he said. 'I'm tellin' you, don't talk like that.'

Mary Ann stared at him. Both in voice and manner he could have been her da at this moment. Her lips trembled; she felt alone, lost. Mr. Lord no longer required her company, and her da had gone from her, and now Corny turning on her. Well, she wasn't going to put up with it, she wasn't. She cried at him, 'Why shouldn't I talk like that? It's the truth.'

'It may be, but I don't like to hear you taking that tack.'

'You don't, do you? . . . Well, for your information, I'd better remind you we're in nineteen-sixty-four, and I would also remind you that you're supposed to have been around a bit . . . America and all over the . . .'

'I don't care if it's twenty-and-sixty-four.' His voice had a rasping edge to it. 'And yes, I've been around a bit, scoff as much as you like, but I've been around more than you have, and when I was . . . around America I didn't hear the girls, at least not the ones I mixed with, saying things like that. If you were still living in Mulhattan's Hall, or over our way in Howden, and you hadn't had your fancy education, it would be understandable.'

Mary Ann's neck and face were scarlet. Her wide eyes were smarting, and her trembling lips moved with soundless words a number of times before she whimpered, 'You can think what you like about me, I don't care, I don't care, only I know it's true what I've said; it could happen. As for the girls in America not talking like that, don't ... don't make me la ... laugh.' Choking on the last words, she gave a demonstration of laughter by bursting into tears. And when he caught her close, crying, 'There! There! Give over.' 'I'm sorry,' she gabbled, 'I'm worried. I'm frightened. I know it could happen. I do, I do. And you ... you going for me and making me out to be something nasty just because I said what ... what I know she's trying to ...'

'There! There! All right, all right. Come on, don't cry. And you're right. Listen ... listen to me.' He lifted her face upwards. 'I know you're right, but somehow ... well!' he moved his head slowly – 'I hate to hear you talk like that. Let everybody else in the world say what they want to say, and how they want to say it, but you ... aw.' He hunched his shoulders. 'Here, dry your face.'

Clumsily he wiped the tears from her face, then said, 'Come on, smile. You don't want to go in and give your mother something else to worry about, do you? She's got enough on her plate at present. Come on.' His mouth twisted sideways as he ended, sanctimoniously, 'Let us be a comfort to her in her old age, anyway.'

Mary Ann hiccoughed; the tears were still rolling from her eyes but she wanted to laugh, and she actually did laugh when, bending down to her, he whispered, 'About the American girls, that was a pack of lies. Coo! The things that some of them used to say, they made you sizzle, like water on a hot frying pan.'

'Oh, Corny, Corny, you're daft. Oh, you are daft.'

They were hurrying up the road now, close once again, and as they neared the farm the dull clouds parted and the sun shone, picking out the newly pink-cement-dashed farmhouse, with its two ornamental red-bricked chimneys straining upwards towards an overhanging branch of a mighty oak tree whose base boarded the road some yards away. It picked out the farm building, white-washed and neat, forming three sides of a square. It showed two farm cottages with their long gardens patterned with vegetables and early chrysanthemums.

As they entered the farm gates there was a murmuring of cattle from the byres, the sharp bark of the dog, and the distant thud of a galloping horse sporting in the field beyond the buildings.

This, her home, had always been a form of heaven to Mary Ann, but now she was experiencing the knowledge that surroundings only become significant when the people close to you are at peace. But there was no peace either in or between those close to her, and the reason for that state was now coming across the courtyard.

Mary Ann did not call to Mike or hurry to greet him, or he to her. As she took in the fact that he was hesitating in the middle of the yard she felt Corny's swift decision, almost as if he had said aloud, 'Well, somebody's got to stand by him.' 'I'll be with you in a minute,' was what he said to her, and as he went towards her father she made her way slowly towards the house.

CHAPTER TWO

MARY ANN woke up with the sun streaming on to her face,
and she blinked into it; then, turning completely over on to
her stomach, she stretched one leg after the other and lay
supine for some moments. Her mind not yet disturbed by
thoughts, she felt relaxed and warm ... and nice, but the
more she tried to hold the feeling the faster she was becoming awake. As she wondered what time it was, she raised
her head and looked at the bedside clock. Half-past seven.
She twisted round and pulled herself upwards by putting her
hands behind her head and gripping the bed rail, then, leaning back and staring into the sun once more, she began to
pick up the sounds from below her. She heard the even note
of her mother's voice, then the deeper tone of Michael's,
then came a short, thick spray of words, the tone of which
she had not heard before rising from the kitchen at this time
of the morning. It brought her upright in the bed; she had
forgotten for the moment that Corny had slept here last
night. They had all, except her father, stayed up late talking
about the wedding, and when Corny was ready to go it was
blowing a gale. It was her mother who had said, 'You can't
go out in this, you'll get soaked.' As usual, Corny had his
motor-bike with him but he hadn't a cape. He hadn't taken
much persuading to stay and he had phoned a fish-and-chip
shop that was three doors away from his home and asked a
neighbour to tell his mother that he was staying the night.

Mary Ann smiled to herself; it would be funny going
down and seeing Corny at breakfast. She had better get up.
She threw the clothes back and sat on the edge of the bed
and again she stretched – she hadn't to go to the office today.
She had taken the day off to help get things ready for the
morrow, and Sarah's wedding. That's why she had felt so
nice, she supposed, when she woke up, not having to go

into work. But the niceness hadn't lasted very long, had it, because now she was feeling as she had done for weeks, worried. Well, she sighed, she wasn't the only one, everyone in the house was worried. ... And yet that wasn't true. Michael wasn't really worried about what was going on; nor was Sarah. They both seemed already to be living separate lives, a joint separate life. And they were chary about discussing the business of her da and Yvonne Radley. Sarah, because she had become very fond of Mike, and Michael, Mary Ann knew, because he wanted to preserve the picture of her da that he had built up around him these last few years. He didn't want to go back to his childhood and the feeling of hate he'd had for the man who couldn't stop drinking. Michael and her da had become very close during the last few years, and now he was shutting his eyes to anything that would show up her da in an unfavourable light. ... She wished that she, too, could shut her eyes to it.

A few minutes later, when she went into the bathroom, she found all the towels wet. That was their Michael; he not only used his own towel but everybody else's. She felt she wanted to rush to the stair-head and cry, as she sometimes did, 'Not a dry towel again! You leave my towel alone, our Michael.' But as she looked in the mirror she said to herself, 'Stop it, there's enough trouble.' Yet she still asked her reflection, 'But why does he want to use so many towels?'

Ten minutes later, as she descended the stairs, she paused for a second when she saw Mike crossing the hall. He was going out the front way and he had his big boots on. ... He was just doing it to aggravate her mother, for her mother took pride in the hall and it always looked lovely.

When she reached the bottom stair Mike had pulled the front door open, and he turned towards her, and after a second, during which he looked hard at her, he said, 'Mornin'.'

'Good morning, Da.'

'Mary Ann.' His voice was low.

'Yes, Da?'

He jerked his head and beckoned her to him, and when she stood before him he looked straight at her as he said, 'I should be down in the bottom field around ten, do you think you could spare me a few minutes?'

Her eyes dropped from his. 'I ... I don't know; me mother's got so many things she wants doing and—'

'All right, all right.' He stood stiffly, holding up his hand in a checking movement. 'Don't come if you don't want to; I understand it's a very busy day for everybody.' His tone was sarcastic. 'But just suppose you have a minute or so to spare, I would—' he paused, 'I would be grateful for a word with you.'

She looked up at him. Her da had never talked like this to her in his life, sarcastically, nor had he ever had to ask her to go and have a word with him. He'd always had to push her from him, stop her from having too many words with him. 'I'll be there,' she said.

'Thank you.' The sarcasm was heavy in his tone.

She turned away and went into the kitchen, there to meet her mother's inquiring glance. It was just the flick of Lizzie's eye but it said plainly, 'What did he say? What did he want?'

Mary Ann answered it with, 'I don't want any bacon, Mother, just some cereal.'

'You'd better get a breakfast into you.'

'I don't feel like it.'

Mary Ann now turned her head towards the table and looked at Corny. His eyes were waiting for her. 'Hello,' she said. 'Did you sleep all right?'

Corny grinned as he replied, 'Like a man with a clear conscience.'

'Huh! Aren't we self-righteous.' She sat down opposite to him, and Corny, looking now at Lizzie and his grin widening, said, 'This is the first time I've seen her first thing in the mornin'. Lord, doesn't she look miserable!'

Lizzie smiled faintly at this boy, at this young man, at this big fellow whom she had tried so hard to dislike – this boy who was the last person on earth she would have wanted Mary Ann to marry; this young man who was too big altogether for Mary Ann and whose prospects, on the other hand, were too small for what she wanted for her daughter; this big fellow who was the cause of Mary Ann not marrying

Tony. For years she had set her heart on her daughter becoming the wife of Mr. Lord's grandson and having all the things that that marriage would entail. But apparently it wasn't to be. How many more disappointments in life could she put up with? How much more could she stand and keep sane? Her mind on the last thought had moved away from Mary Ann, and now she was saying to herself, What were they talking about at the front door? . . . And fancy him going out the front way in his dirty boots. He just did that to work me up after last night. As she picked up the teapot she thought, Perhaps I should have let him talk. Yet, listening to him making excuses and giving reasons for his madness would only have made things worse. I couldn't have bore it.

Mary Ann's raised voice brought her attention to the table. 'What's the matter now?' she asked.

'Well, I'm just saying I'm right.' Mary Ann looked up at Lizzie as she pointed a finger of toast across the table in the direction of Corny. 'He said, why do I want to cut up the toast like this and put finicky bits of marmalade on it, and I said it was the right way. And it is, isn't it? Not to butter and marmalade a slice all at once, I mean.'

'Oh, Mary Ann!' Lizzie shook her head at her daughter with a despairing movement. 'Why must you start on such things?'

'But I didn't, Mother, it was him.' She nodded at Corny.

'Huh!' said Corny. 'She was talking as if I didn't know the right way to eat. I know all about fingers of toast and dabbing bits of this, that, and the other on it, but you only do that when you're in hotels, or out with posh company, don't you, Mam?' He addressed Lizzie with the familiar term he had always used since he had become engaged to Mary Ann; and his attitude now towards her was as if she was his mother and arbitrator in a family dispute.

And now Lizzie smiled at him. You couldn't help but like Corny; however much you tried not to, you couldn't help but like him. She nodded at him, saying, 'Yes, you're right, Corny.'

'He's not, Mother. And don't stick up for him about such things, it only makes him worse . . . big-headed.'

27

'Whose going to stick up for whose big head?' The door from the scullery opened and Michael came in. He looked a younger edition of his father, and as he walked down the long room to the table he could have been Mike himself twenty years earlier. When he picked up a slice of toast from the rack and started to butter it, Lizzie said, 'You've had your breakfast not half-an-hour ago.'

'Was it only half-an-hour? It seems I've never had a bite since yesterday.'

'Well, tomorrow's not affecting your appetite, that's something.' Lizzie smiled tenderly at her son, and Michael, reaching out for the marmalade, stopped with his hand in mid air and inquired of Corny, 'What's the matter?'

'Nothing ... nothing.' Corny's voice was rapid. 'Go on, marmalade your toast.'

'Aw you!' Mary Ann, her lips tight now, was shaking her head at the aggravating individual, and when Michael had finished spreading his slice of toast thickly with marmalade, Corny looked at her and gave one wide grin as he let out a deep chest full of air and said, 'There now.'

'There now, what? What's this all about? What's the matter with you two first thing in the morning?'

'She says it ain't—' Corny stressed the ain't, 'she says it ain't refeened to eat toast like that, Michael. We should cut it into refeened little fingers, like so.' He demonstrated.

'Oh, we should, should we?' Michael was returning Corny's grin. 'Oh, what it is to be a lady; it must be painful.' And leaning towards Corny, Michael pityingly added, 'Boy, I don't envy you. . . . Poor blighter. . . '

'Aw, there's a pair of you.' Mary Ann tossed her head disdainfully. 'You eat like pigs, clagging everything up. . . .'

'HA!' A high derisive hoot came from Michael. 'Listen to her. Listen to her. Listen to her. Ooh! Miss Shaughnessy, how can you let yourself down to such a low level? Did you hear what she said, Corny?' He turned wide eyes in Corny's direction again. ' "Clag," she said. Did you hear her? ... Clag.'

'Now, now, stop it, or it'll end up in words, hot words, if not in tears.' Lizzie, addressing the two young men and

28

bringing their eyes towards her, motioned with a jerk of her head towards Mary Ann's back.

'Tears.' Mary Ann rounded on her mother. 'They won't reduce me to tears, not that pair.'

As she bounced up from the table, Lizzie placed a hand on her shoulder and said, 'Sit down and have something to eat. Now you're not going to start doing anything until you have your breakfast.' As she pressed her daughter into the chair again she could have added, as she might have done some weeks earlier, 'What's put you in this tear so early in the morning?' But she had no need to question her daughter's state of mind, she knew the reason only too well.

Although Lizzie's own nerves were near to breaking point, and her heart was sore, and her feelings towards her husband were almost verging on hate at this moment, she wished Mary Ann had not taken a stand against her father, for her attitude towards the man she had always adored seemed to Lizzie to put a finality on the whole thing. Nothing Mike had ever done in his life had made Mary Ann stop speaking to him, until now, and Lizzie found her feelings entwining round her daughter, loving her as she had not done for some time, in fact, since she was a baby, because since Mary Ann had come to the use of reason she had always taken her father's part. Be he in the right or wrong – and he was more often in the wrong than not – Mary Ann had always stood valiantly by him. But Mary Ann was no longer a child, she was almost twenty and she was soon to be married, and in her father's present madness she was seeing him for the first time as he really was. Yet in spite of all this Lizzie wanted to say to her: 'Go and talk to him; be kind to him, because I can't.' And, knowing her husband, she knew that he needed somebody ... he always needed somebody to be kind to him.

At this moment there came the sound of fumbling with the handle of the door leading from the hall, and although all their eyes turned in the direction of the door no one got up to open it, and it was seconds later before it was pushed wide, and there entered Sarah Flanagan.

Sarah was supporting herself on two elbow crutches, and while her right foot tentatively touched the ground she dragged the whole of her left leg from the hip downwards as if it was part of a dead carcass that had been tied to her. From the waist up she was well formed, and above the long neck was a radiant face.

This was the Sarah Flanagan who had lived opposite to Mary Ann in Mulhattan's Hall for years. This was the girl who had been Mary Ann's enemy, who had fought with her daily, playing on her weak point, her affection for her drunken father. This was the girl who had written things about Mike Shaughnessy on walls and had driven Mary Ann to a frenzy of retaliation. This was the girl who had found, at an early age, that she loved horses and wanted to work with them, and had worked with them until two years ago when she had been struck with polio. But above all, this was the girl who loved Michael Shaughnessy and whom Michael Shaughnessy adored. There was no resemblance between this wise, tender, beautiful cripple, and the girl who had been brought up in Burton Street.

No one in the room moved to help her until she almost reached the table; then Michael went quietly to her side and pulled out a chair for her, and when she was seated they looked at each other for a moment. It was the look that always brought an odd feeling into Mary Ann's body. Mary Ann, it could be said now, also loved Sarah as much as she had once hated her. And although they had scrapped all their lives, she also loved Michael. Yet when she saw Sarah and Michael together there emanated a feeling from them that created in her a sense of want, and of loss. For what exactly, she didn't know; she told herself it was because they never fought, but seemed always at peace in each other's company, whereas she and Corny rarely met unless they went for each other in some way.

'Sleep well?' Michael was asking Sarah; and she answered with a shake of her head. 'No, hardly at all. . . .' She paused, then asked, 'Did you?'

Michael, bowing his head as if in shame, tried to suppress a smile as he confessed, 'Like a top.'

'They have no finer feelings, that's why they can sleep.' Mary Ann was looking at Sarah, and Sarah answered, 'Perhaps you're right. Or no nerves.' She cast a swift glance again towards Michael, and he, bending and kissing her quite unselfconsciously, said softly, 'I'll move my coarse presence from you to the cow sheds.'

As Michael went to leave the kitchen Corny asked, 'Give you a hand or anything, Michael?' And Michael, turning from the doorway, answered, 'We never say no to an extra hand, Corny, but I thought you'd have to be at the garage.'

'No, I took a couple of days off,' said Corny. 'And for no other reason, mind you' – he was nodding his head now at Michael – 'but that Miss Shaughnessy had done the same and she'd be lonely without me. . . . Wouldn't know what to do with herself, in fact.'

Michael was laughing, Sarah was laughing, but Mary Ann, refusing to smile, was giving Corny a straight stare as he, rising from the table, bent towards her and chucked her under the chin, saying with tenderness that was more real than make-believe, 'Good-bye, sugar.'

When the door had closed on the two young men Mary Ann let her face slide into a smile, and when she looked at Sarah they both began to laugh.

Lizzie sat down at the table, poured herself out a cup of tea, and, looking at her daughter, remarked, 'Your breakfasts, in the future, should be very entertaining.'

'Well, he's so aggravating.'

'And you're not, of course.' Lizzie's remark was softened by the tilt of her lips. 'In some ways I think he's very patient with you.'

'Patient! Huh!' Mary Ann tossed her head, while at the same time feeling pleased that her mother was taking Corny's part. She wanted her mother to like Corny, for she felt that even after all this long time of knowing him, and accepting him as her future son-in-law, she was still in two minds about him.

But her attention was drawn to Sarah, who was saying, 'Breakfasts in the future are going to be different for me; I'll miss all this . . . the talk . . . the bustle.' She looked at Lizzie as she spoke, and Lizzie replied softly, 'I'll miss you, too. It won't be the same without you, Sarah.'

As her mother and her future sister-in-law exchanged

warm glances there was wafted to Mary Ann that feeling of want, of loss. Her mother liked Sarah, and this fact alone said a great deal, because Lizzie adored her son, and Sarah was marrying that son . . . taking him away.

Sarah was now saying, 'It's funny how your opinions change. A year ago I was dead against going into the bungalow, wasn't I? And so was Michael, although his reasons were different from mine. He didn't want to be beholden to Mr. Lord, whereas I didn't want to be stuck helpless in a house away from you all. But now—' her smile widened and lit up the whole of her face, 'now I can get about, it's different. . . . And fancy me being able to drive a car. You would never have believed it a year ago, would you?'

'No,' said Lizzie. 'You never would, Sarah. It's like a miracle.'

Yes, thought Mary Ann, what had happened to Sarah was like a miracle. When she came to take up the front room here it was with the idea of her and Michael marrying almost straight away, and then one day she announced, and quite calmly, that she wasn't going to marry Michael until she could walk. Her decision had caused a bit of an upheaval at the time and a great number of shaking heads. But tomorrow Sarah would achieve the goal she had aimed at, she would go up to the altar rails on her feet. In a white wedding gown that would cover her trailing limb, she would stand by Michael's side while they were married.

Remembering the work, the patience, yes, and the tears that Sarah had endured to achieve her object, there now attached itself to that odd feeling in Mary Ann one of inadequacy. She felt useless, utterly useless. She had never done anything. When Mrs. McBride's words of yesterday came to her, she said to herself, Aw, what's that? Mrs. McBride was just trying to be nice. And as she rose abruptly from the table she wished that something awful would happen so that she could prove herself like Sarah had.

'Where you off to in a rush?' Lizzie looked at her sharply.

'Nowhere. I just wanted to make a start. . . . Shall I do the dishes and clear the scullery?'

'Yes. Yes, you could do that.'

As she stood at the sink washing the dishes and the murmur of her mother's and Sarah's voices came to her, she thought, Why don't they get up and get going? She said there was so much to do – that's why I stayed off the day. . . . When her hands became still in the soapy water she looked down at them and said to herself, I don't feel nice inside, I don't. . . . It's awful, awful feeling like this.

At half-past nine Mary Ann was wondering what excuse she could make in order to leave the house and go down to the bottom field. And then her mother made it plain sailing for her by saying, 'Will you take the tea out to them?' She did not say to your da. 'They're in the bottom field I think.'

Taking the basket loaded with three lidded cans of tea and a cellophane bag of substantial cheese sandwiches, she left the house by the back door, then cut across the farmyard, calling to Simon as she did so. She touched the Labrador's head as he took up his position close to her side, and when they went through the gate and on to the field path a long-haired black cat jumped from a low hayrick and joined them. The cat mewed and she stooped and patted it, saying, 'All right, Tigger.' Then they moved on, the dog close to her side and the cat trotting behind them.

When they reached the low wall that bordered the south meadow Sarah's horse – which she was determined to ride one day – threw up its head and came galloping towards them, and when, neighing as it went, it trotted at the other side of the wall, Mary Ann called to him, 'When I come back, Dusty, when I come back.' When they reached the end of the wall the horse, unable to go further, neighed loudly as they went down a steep cart track towards a large field, where, in the far distance, she could see the binder, driven by Michael, turning in the direction of Corny, who was at the other end of the line. But she couldn't see her da. She walked towards where the ground rose before drooping into a miniature valley, and as she neared it Mike came into view.

On the sight of him the dog gave one staccato bark, and Mike turned his head, then straightened his back, and as they approached the dog left Mary Ann's side and went quietly forward and nuzzled him.

'I've brought your break.' She was looking down into the basket.

'I'm ready for it.' He held out his hand, and she handed him one of the cans.

'Come and sit down a minute.' He pointed to a hillock of ground, but she answered quickly, 'I've got to take theirs; it'll . . . it'll get cold.'

'It can wait a few minutes.' His gaze, fixed on her face, brought her eyes up to his and she went and sat down.

When Mike lowered himself to the ground, but not too near her, the dog lay down against his side, while the cat, thinking it was about time to show some remnants of her independence, strolled, delicate-pawed, over the stubbly grass along the hedgerow.

Taking the lid off the can, Mike drank thirstily. After replacing the lid and setting the can on the ground, he wiped his broad mouth with the pad of his thumb; then, pulling up his knees, he rested his forearm on them, and, his head going slightly back, he looked up into the wide, high sky before saying gruffly, 'What's come over you and me, Mary Ann?'

When she made no answer, except to lower her head, he, with his eyes still turned skywards, went on, 'I thought nothin' on God's earth could come atween us. I would have sworn that if I'd committed a murder you would have stood by me.'

'And I would.' Her words were scarcely audible to him. 'You know I would. . . . But this isn't a murder, it's something different . . . something . . .' She paused for a long while before adding in a thin whisper, 'Nasty.'

'Aw, my God, Mary Ann!' He was no longer looking skywards; his head had drooped and his brow was resting on his clenched fist, and his face became contorted as he ground his strong teeth. Then, raising his head slightly from his hands, he muttered, 'You don't know. And how should you? You can't understand; things happen. You don't ask for them to happen, you don't want them to happen, they happen in little episodes. Aye, that's how they happen, in little episodes. And I can tell you this. . . .' He turned his head slightly in her direction. 'They would stay little episodes if

34

people would leave them alone, if they would stop making issues out of them; stop keeping on, if they would forget them, or just take them as part and parcel of life. Then they wouldn't grow. You understand what I'm saying now?' His head was fully turned towards her, waiting for her answer, and she turned hers and looked at him. She understood what he was saying. The people he was referring to were simply her mother; but she didn't blame her mother for the attitude she had taken, how could she? Very likely she would react in the same way herself if Corny were to carry on with another girl. . . . Oh, she would go on worse than her mother, she knew that. Her mother could be cool, and distant, staving off words. . . . She paused here in her thinking. Perhaps that attitude was worse than having it out, having a row. Yes, she knew it was.

'Look, Mary Ann, I've done nothing wrong.' Mike's voice was quiet and level now. 'You understand what I mean, don't you?'

'Yes, Da.' She gave a small nod. 'Yes, I understand. But how long will you be able to say that?' She was amazed at herself for asking such a question, of her da of all people.

'Mary Ann.' Mike closed his eyes now and rocked his big head in wide, slow movements. 'It's a passing phase, it'll blow over.'

'Why did you start it?'

'Why does a man breathe? You don't know . . . it's one of those things.' He turned and looked over the wide field to where the binder was now coming towards them, and he said, as if to himself, 'Life gallops on, and the quicker it gallops the more set it gets. And sometimes in the night you get frightened – aye, frightened; you're done for, finished, you're old. And then along comes somebody who makes you feel a lad again, and you like it. You get a new lease of life, it's like a drug. And you've got enough sense in the back of your mind to recognize it as just that, an' you know damn well that its effects will wear off. But for the time being you're living like you thought you would never live again. . . . Aw, it's all too complicated. . . .'

Mary Ann, her own hands clasped tightly now, was thinking, Mrs. McBride, that's what Mrs. McBride had said. At least, her words had meant the same thing. She was wise, was Mrs. McBride. But then she was very old; whereas her mother wasn't old enough to be wise in that way yet, and her da was being cruel to her. He was indulging in a second childhood. Well, anyway, a second youth, and not thinking about the effects on her mother ... or the effect on herself. This thought forced from her mouth the words, 'She's younger than me, Da.'

As Mike began to beat his brow with his clenched fist, Mary Ann rose slowly to her feet, and when she went to pass him his hand shot out and pulled her close to him. Her face just above his, they stared at each other. Looking at him, Mary Ann did not think as she had done from a child, He's handsome, me da, and there's something about him. Years ago she had been flattered when women like Mrs. Quinton had liked her da, but not any more. Her eyes now took in his neck. It was thick, and brown, and had lines on it; and there was hair sprouting from within his ears. Her da was no longer a young man, he was in his forties. Never before had she thought like this about him, she had always seen him young.

'Are you listening to me?'

She blinked twice. 'Yes, Da.'

'I said, it would be over the morrow.'

'What?'

'You weren't listening ... I said it'll be finished the morrow.'

'Oh, Da.' Slowly she smiled at him. 'You'll tell them ...?' She did not think of the girl alone in this matter; her mother was a force to be contended with also, and she was fully aware of this. 'When they come to the wedding, you'll tell them?'

'Well ...' He moved his full lips one over the other and lowered his gaze for a moment, before saying, 'There ... there won't be any need to tell them, but it'll be finished, you'll see.'

'But, Da. . . .'

'Believe me.' He cupped her cheek with his hand. 'Don't worry any more; it'll be over the morrow night, you'll see. I promise you that.'

She believed him. She knew he meant it. She wanted to burst into tears and fall against him, burying her head in the beloved neck. She gulped and, lowering her head, turned from him, saying, 'All right, Da, all right.'

Mike made no further move to detain her, but as she hurried across the field Corny's voice hailed her, shouting, 'Hie there!' But it did not turn her round. For answer, she began to run, the tears raining unchecked now down her face. Her feet slipping on the stubbles, she ran until she reached the car track, and it was as she was crossing this that another voice came to her from where the track joined the road leading to the farm. And there she saw Tony's car, and Tony himself waving to her.

Aw, what was she to do? If she didn't go down to him he would turn back to the house and find out what was wrong with her. She rubbed her face hastily with her handkerchief and, walking slowly now, went down the slope towards the car.

As Tony came to meet her she could see Lettice leaning from the car window, and as she answered Lettice's salute with a lift of her hands, Tony came up to her, saying, 'What's the matter? What are you crying for?'

'Leave me alone.' She could talk like this to Tony.

'Well—' he smiled ruefully, 'to use your own phraseology, Miss, nobody's touching you.'

'Aw, don't be clever or facetious, I can't stand it this morning.' She had for a long while now stopped thinking, with regard to Tony, I could have married him if I'd liked, because she knew that Tony wasn't for her, or she for him. Lettice was the right one for Tony. She might be a bit older but she was what he needed.

'Hello, Mary Ann.' Lettice opened the door and stepped into the road.

'Hello, Lettice.'

Lettice now bent towards her, saying softly, 'What's the matter?'

'Oh . . .' Mary Ann shook her head. 'You know what it is.'

As Lettice remained silent, Tony put in, 'You're still worrying about Mike?'

'Wouldn't you? If you were in my place ... or me mother's?'

As Tony raised his brows, Lettice put in, 'Of course he would, but at the same time, Mary Ann, I can't imagine your father doing anything really stupid. He's flattered by the girl; men are made like that.'

If anybody had experience about men being flattered by girls it was Lettice. She had suffered from it for years, putting a face on things to keep her first marriage together, and what had happened in the end?

'Some men,' went on Lettice, with a knowing quality in her voice, 'would let it go to their heads, but not Mike.'

In the pause that followed, Tony put in, lightly, 'I saw Michael earlier on this morning. He appeared as calm as a cucumber, quite unconcerned.'

Mary Ann gave a little smile at this, saying, 'Our Michael doesn't give much away. I heard him moving about in his room at two o'clock this morning. Yet he told Sarah he slept like a top, and made her believe it.'

Lettice and Tony laughed, then Tony said, 'I've got a message for you ... he wants to see you.'

There was no need for Mary Ann to question the 'he'; there was only one he ... Mr. Lord. 'What does he want?' she asked.

Tony shook his head. 'I don't know.'

Mary Ann stared up into the thin face that was so like Mr. Lord's, and she said, 'Of course you know; there's nothing you don't know. ... He does know, doesn't he, Lettice?'

Confronted with the question, the older woman said, 'Leave me out of this, Mary Ann. But I can tell you this, he's in good spirits this morning.'

'That's a change,' said Mary Ann. 'What's brought it on?'

'Oh ...' Lettice looked from Mary Ann to her husband, then back to Mary Ann as she said, 'He had a bit of news last night that seemed to please him. He's ... he's hoping for a great-grandson.'

Mary Ann's mouth dropped open as she turned her gaze towards Tony, but Tony was looking at Lettice. Lettice was going to have a baby, but she was old. ... Oh well, not really

38

... but old to have a baby. She was over thirty-six. Well, people had babies up to forty and after, didn't they? She supposed so, but somehow ... well, it didn't seem quite right. Lettice herself was a grandmother. Her only daughter, whom she rarely saw, had had a baby last year.

Both Lettice and Tony were looking at her now, and she made her smile broad as she said, 'Oh, that'll be lovely for you. Fancy you going to have a baby. ... Do you want a baby?'

Lettice's attractive face puckered as if in doubt; and then she said, 'Not ... not particularly, Mary Ann, but I have two men to please, and both of them seem bent on it. The old one more than the young one, I must confess.' She now lent her head gently towards Tony, and he put his arm around her and pressed her to him. And Mary Ann thought, I wish they wouldn't do that. And this was strange, because never had she witnessed affection between her da and her mother without finding joy in it. When they were happy she wanted the whole world to be happy, but when, as now, they weren't happy she supposed she resented other people's happiness. And yet she'd had a large hand in bringing happiness to Tony and Lettice, so she shouldn't feel like this.

She said quickly, 'Eeh! I'll have to be going, there's so much to do. ... But I'm glad for you, I am, I am. ... Will you call it Mary Ann if it's a girl?'

'Not on your life. Fancy another like you!' Tony pushed at her with the flat of his hand as he laughed, then added seriously, 'You will go up, won't you?'

'Yes, I'll go up. ... Imagine what would happen if I disobeyed the order.'

'Yes, imagine.'

'And you won't tell me what it's about?'

'I told you, I don't know.' He was grinning at her now.

'Oh, go on.' She turned from him, then turned back again, saying swiftly, 'Bye-bye, Lettice.'

'Bye-bye, Mary Ann.'

Mary Ann did not give her mother Lettice's news, because she felt that Lizzie would consider it should be her to whom this news should apply, and so would cry. What she did say to Lizzie was, 'I saw Tony and Lettice going out in the car. Tony said Mr. Lord wants me.'

'What for? Did he say?'

'He said he didn't know, but I'm sure he does.'

'Well, you'd better get yourself off, hadn't you?'

'But there's all those cakes to ice.'

'Never mind about them, get yourself away up.'

Her mother always saw to it that Mr. Lord's orders were obeyed, at least as far as it lay within her power, and she added now, 'Don't dawdle, you don't know what he might want to see you about.'

'Well, it can't be anything that's going to go bad for an hour or so, can it?'

'Mary Ann!'

'All right, all right, I'll go now.'

Once again Mary Ann went through the farmyard, but this time she turned up the hill towards the big house that stood on the brow. She went through the paved courtyard, with its ornamental urns of flowers, to the back door, and, after knocking, she opened the door and entered the kitchen.

A middle-aged woman, turning from the Aga stove, said brightly, 'Good morning, miss.'

'Good morning, Eva . . . Ben about?'

'I think he's with the master, miss.'

The advent of a woman servant in Mr. Lord's house, and in Ben's kitchen, in itself spoke volumes for Lettice's power.

As she left the kitchen, Ben, his old head sunk into his hollowed shoulders, came shambling across the hall. He had a small tray in his hand, on which was an empty glass and plate, and on the sight of Mary Ann he put the tray on the side table and, turning to her, said in a hoarse whisper, 'He's waiting for you. He's in high fettle this morning.' His wrinkled face moved into what for him was a smile, and Mary Ann, bending towards him, whispered, 'What does he want, do you know, Ben?'

It wasn't strange that Mary Ann should ask Ben this question, because Ben knew everything. Ben had lived with the taciturn Mr. Lord for as far back as he cared to remember, and although his master treated him at times as a numskull, to Ben he was God, all the God he needed.

The small smile still on his face, Ben said, 'You'll know soon enough. Go on, don't keep him waiting.'

When Mary Ann entered the drawing-room, Mr. Lord was sitting in his favourite position before the tall windows, looking out on to the terraced gardens. He was a tall man, thin as a rake, with skin wizened almost as much as that of his servant, but his pale-blue eyes held a brightness and vitality that denied his age.

'You've taken your time.' The voice was stern, the face unsmiling, and to this greeting Mary Ann said, 'Well, Tony only told me not more than fifteen minutes ago; I can't fly.'

A quiver passed over the wrinkled skin, and the eyes, from under lowered lids, looked keenly at her as he said, 'In a bad mood this morning, aren't you?'

'Me in a bad mood?' Her eyes stretched wide, and on this he held up his hand, saying, 'All right, all right, we won't go into it. . . . Everybody very busy, I suppose?' His voice held a quiet note now.

'Yes.' She sat down in front of him. He always demanded that she sit in front of him, where he could look fully at her.

'And everybody on edge?'

She nodded at him, then said, 'All except Sarah and Michael.'

He smiled, and the wrinkles on his face converged together. And then his head nodding slowly, he said, 'They'll be happy, those two. Although he's taken on a burden, it'll become lighter, not heavier, with the years, and as she works at her miracle she'll weave wonder into their lives. . . . Don't you think so?'

The pale, steely gaze was tight on her face, and she answered abruptly, 'I don't know.' And she didn't know, because she wasn't thinking of Michael or Sarah. But she knew this old man, she knew that his mind was really not on Sarah and Michael's future, but was working in another direction.

His eyes still hard on her, his lips moving as if he were

41

sucking on a sweet, he stared at her for a full minute before inquiring, 'What's the matter with you? You're upset.'

If Mary Ann knew her Mr. Lord, Mr. Lord knew his Mary Ann.

'I'm not. What makes you think that?'

'You always were a big liar, my dear, but you were also a bad liar. What's troubling you? I ask you, what's troubling you?'

'I tell you, nothing. But we're all in a rush down there.' She motioned her head backwards towards the window, indicating the farmhouse. 'We . . . we don't have a wedding every day.'

Again the pale-blue eyes were holding hers. And now Mr. Lord said, 'It's Mike, isn't it? . . . Oh! oh! don't get on your high horse.' He now bent his stiff body towards her and said softly, 'I know that look in your face, and only your father can put it there. He's done so before and he's doing it now, and I've no doubt but he'll do it again many times before you die.'

'I tell you . . .'

'You can go on telling me, but what I want to hear is what he has been up to now.'

'Nothing, nothing.' That would be the last straw if Mr. Lord heard about Yvonne Radley. Oh, Holy Mother – a section of her mind was praying now – don't let him find out about that.

'If you don't tell me I can find out. I have my ways and means.' He was nodding quickly at her. 'Tony and Lettice just tell me what they think is good for me, but if I want to know anything I have my ways and means.' His head was moving slower now, and Mary Ann thought, Yes, he has his ways and means. Ben was his ways and means. She liked Ben, and Ben, she knew, liked her; surprisingly, because Ben had no thought but for this old man here, and that his days should be spent in peace and free from worry. But to achieve this she knew that Ben, even in his doddering old age, would take on the task of the C.I.D. to find out anything his master needed to know. But Mary Ann thought none the less of Ben for this, she only feared what his probing might do to her da, because, besides trying to rule her life, Mr. Lord had also tried to rule Mike's, and her father wasn't as easy under the reins as she was. Not that she was really easy.

'Well, have it your own way.' Mr. Lord leaned back and rested his head against the wing of the chair, and, after drawing in a long thin breath and placing his bony fingertips together, he said, 'How would you like me to do something for that big fellow of yours?'

Mary Ann's eyes were completely round now, and, knowing the other thing he had done for Corny, which had transported him to the other side of the world, she was wary in her answer. 'It all depends on what it is,' she said.

'Yes, that's a good answer: it all depends on what it is. Well . . . how would you like to see him set up in a garage, a real garage?'

'But . . . but he's after the one in Moor Lane.'

Mr. Lord jerked his head disdainfully. 'That isn't a garage, that's a broken-down repair shop, and on a side road at that. What business can he expect there?'

'They're thinking of opening it up, making it a main . . .'

'Yes, yes, in twenty years' time. I know all about that. . . . But there's a place going now, at least shortly, on the main road . . . Baxter's.'

'Baxter's!' Her mouth now formed an elongated O, and when she closed it she swallowed before repeating, 'Baxter's! But it's a show place.'

'I grant you it's a show place. But it also does a very good business.'

'Oh.' She was smiling. 'You'd really set him up in that?'

He nodded. 'Yes, I would. I feel I owe him something for that little trip he made on my suggestion. Baxter's will be in the market in three months' time. I intend to buy it and lease it to him, and if he shows progress I'll give him a share in it, in a year or so. I think that is a fair enough deal, don't you?'

'Oh, yes . . . yes.' Her words were slow. It was wonderful. She said now, 'He's got quite a bit of his own saved up, over four hundred.'

'Four hundred! Huh!' Mr. Lord's tone was now derisive. 'What do you think can be done with four hundred, Mary

43

Ann, when you want to buy a business of this kind? Baxter's will go for nothing less than thirty thousand . . . thirty thousand pounds!'

Her face was straight. She couldn't visualize the enormous sum of thirty thousand pounds and the potentialities therein, but she could see the great achievement, and what could be done with four hundred pounds because she had helped in the gathering of it. When Corny would say on a Saturday night, 'Shall we go down to the bowling alley in Jarrow?' she would think for a moment: if they went to the bowling alley it would mean anything up to two pounds spent in the evening. So time and time again she had said, 'Oh, let's just go for a run on the bike.' And sitting on the pillion, clinging tightly to him, she had spent wind-torn, chilling hours, to enable them to add to the growing sum on which their future was to be built.

'You must be realistic, Mary Ann. Businesses are not bought in hundreds today, it takes thousands, tens of thousands to get a start, that is if you want to make real money and not peddle your life away in a backwater.'

The backwater he was referring to was, she knew, Meyer's garage in Moor Lane.

'You're pleased, aren't you?' It was a question, and she forced herself to smile as she answered, 'Oh, yes, yes. And it's kind of you.'

'Don't be a hypocrite.' He was sitting upright again. 'You don't think it's kind of me at all. You don't like the idea that your Cornelius can't buy a motor-concern with his four hundred. . . . Am I right?'

She did not reply for a moment, but her head wagged just the slightest. And then, getting to her feet, she said, 'Yes, you are right, because he's worked hard to save it and—'

'Doubtless, doubtless. And I like to hear it, it's a promising trait in him; it could get him far, the saving trait, but not four hundred, not in the car business, not in this day and age. The days of the Morris miracles are over. But your future husband, Mary Ann, has, I think, a head on his shoulders and he won't be so foolish as to look a gift horse in the mouth. . . . Now will you go and tell him that I would like to see him? I understand he is on the farm, and' – he raised a finger to her – 'I would like to think that his reception of my offer will be a little more enthusiastic than yours.'

'I'm sorry ... I know it's good of you and I'm grateful, I really am.' She moved towards the chair and placed her hand on his, to find it immediately gripped, and she was almost brought to tears for the second time that morning when, his face softening, he said, 'I want to do things for you, Mary Ann. I want to see you settled with all the comforts and amenities which would have been yours if you had come into this house. I have grown very fond of Lettice ... yes, I have, which is just as well, for it helps to oil the wheels of living together, but Lettice will never be you, my dear. ... I've thought recently that you might have imagined that you were being shut out, but no, no. And I thought I must do something to prove to you that that'll never happen. And then, when I learned yesterday that I may in the near future be presented with a great-grandchild, I was pleased, and when one is pleased one thinks about other people, and as you, my dear, are never very far from my mind, I thought, I'll celebrate.' He squeezed her hand. 'And what better way to celebrate than by acquiring a garage.'

There was a lump wedged tightly in her gullet. Oh, he was good, good, he always had been; aggravating, dominating, an old devil at times, but good. Swiftly, she bent forward and pressed her face to his while holding his other cheek with her hand. When, turning quickly from him, she went to leave the room, he checked her quietly, saying, 'Tell Cornelius I want to see him.'

She hurried through the kitchen with her face averted from both Ben and Eva, and then she was running down the hill. When she came to the low stone wall she mounted its broad top and, looking over the fields to where, in the far distance, she saw the figures of Michael and Corny, and her da, she put her fingers into her mouth and blew a sharp high whistle that could have been the envy of many a boy, and when she saw the faces turn towards her she cupped her mouth in her hands and called, 'Cor-NY! Here ... here!' When she felt she had his attention, she beckoned him with a wide wave of her arm.

She saw Corny break away at a trot and take the field in long, loping strides. She saw him jump the other end of the stone wall, and then he was coming up the steep incline, still running, towards her.

When he reached her he stood for a moment, panting; then exclaimed, laughingly, 'Coo! That would get you in training. . . . You want me?' His face wore a broad grin, and before she had time to reply, he added, 'A whistling woman and a crowing hen is neither good for God nor man . . . that's what me mother says.'

'Perhaps your mother's right.'

He narrowed his eyes at her as he stooped down and, looking searchingly into her face, asked, 'What's up? You been crying?'

'No.' She jerked her chin to the side. 'You've got to go and see Mr. Lord.'

'Who, me? What for?'

'Because he wants you to . . . that's all.' The downward movement of her chin now lent emphasis to the words.

'When he wants me it doesn't mean good. I don't trust that old boy, and never will.' He straightened up and pushed his shoulders back.

'Now, Corny, stop it. It is for your good . . . for our good.'

'Ah . . . ah. Here we go. . . . Well, what is it?' His expression changed.

As she stared up into his stiff, straight face she decided that if he was to obey Mr. Lord's command she'd better keep Mr. Lord's proposal to herself. She knew her Corny. His mind was full of odd values, odd ideas. You never knew but that he might turn down the offer if it wasn't put to him right. She lied unblinkingly as she said, 'If I knew what he wanted you for wouldn't I tell you? He just said he wanted to see you.'

Corny wrinkled his big nose. 'I don't like it. He's hardly spoken to me since I came back from America.'

'Can you blame him? You shut him up before he started by telling him that you wanted help from nobody and that you were going to join the band.'

'Aye, yes, I did.' At the memory, a smile twisted Corny's

46

lips. 'And I remember he said that all I'd have to live on would be the hot air that was left over from blowing my cornet. He's sharp, is the old boy.'

'And he was right. That's all you would have had to live on if you'd taken up with the band again. They went flat . . . in more ways than one.'

'That's because they hadn't me with them.' As he brought his fist along the point of her chin, she said softly, 'Go on, Corny. And don't aggravate him.' She caught at his hand. 'He's old.'

'All right.' He gripped both her hands now and went to pull her towards him, but Mary Ann, noting the deep, tender look in his eyes, protested swiftly, 'Eeh! no, Corny. Now stop it, there's Jonesy down in that field.'

'He won't mind.'

'Don't be daft. . . . Now give over. Ooh!'

She tried vainly to push off his long arms as they went around her, but when her feet left the ground and she was held tightly to him, and his mouth touched hers, she relaxed against him for a moment. And she still leant against him when he released her and she was on her feet again. Then, as was often the case, they turned from each other without a word, for words would only have diminished the depths of feeling between them.

'You're mad . . . daft . . . up the pole.' Mary Ann seemed to grow as she stood facing Corny; and now she twisted her head around and addressed her mother, where Lizzie was toying with her half-finished dinner. 'Isn't he, Ma? Tell him, isn't he mad?'

Lizzie was vitally aware of Mike sitting at the far end of the table, his head bowed over his plate, eating solidly as if all that was going on was no concern of his. But Mary Ann had asked her a question – she had not, as usual, asked it of her da, she had asked her. She turned her head slowly to where Corny stood, seemingly isolated on the edge of the hearth rug, and she forced herself to say what was in her mind, yet the translation of her thoughts were mild, for all she said was, 'I think you're being very foolish, Corny; it's a wonderful offer.'

'Wonderful offer be damned!'

Mike had risen from the table, almost overturning the chair as he did so, and although he had taken up, and repeated, Lizzie's words, it was to Mary Ann that he looked as he barked, 'He's right. And he's told you why he's right; the old man is not doing this for him, he's doing it for you so that when you're married he can still keep the reins on you. . . . You're being foolish!' He was again quoting Lizzie's words, and it was her he was yelling at, her he was getting at, not at Mary Ann, although he levelled his spleen towards her. 'Let him go his own road, make his own decisions. He's made one the day; instead of going for him stand by him. You mightn't have so much ham on it but what you do have will be what he's earned and worked for, it won't come from the backhander that's buying your affections.'

As Mike grabbed up his pipe from the mantelpiece and stalked from the room Lizzie rose slowly from her seat, and she stood, her hands gripping the edge of the table, looking to where Sarah sat with bowed head, and Michael opposite to her chewed on his lower lip.

'See what you've done?' Mary Ann's voice, cracking with temper, turned on Corny, and before he could answer her Michael's clear tone cut in. 'He's done what he thinks is right.'

Michael was also on his feet now, and, looking towards Corny, he said, 'I know how you feel. I felt the same when he first offered us the bungalow. . . .'

'But you took the bungalow, didn't you?' Mary Ann bent her body aggressively towards her brother, and he, his voice rising now, shouted back at her, 'But only on my own terms, not as a gift.'

There was a moment of tense silence when no one moved, but in it Mary Ann noticed the slight quiver attacking Sarah's shoulders, and, contrition swamping her, she bowed her head and murmured, 'I'm sorry . . . I'm sorry, Sarah, I . . . I didn't mean anything.'

'I know, I know.' Sarah's hand moved out in Mary Ann's direction, and Mary Ann, going towards her, said, 'All this carry-on and your wedding the morrow.'

'That makes no difference. . . . Would you hold the chair?'

Mary Ann held the back of the chair firmly while Sarah gripped the table and pulled herself to her feet; then looking towards Michael, she said softly, 'Have you a minute? I've packed that case but I can't close it.'

Without a word Michael went towards the door leading into the hall, and holding it open, waited until Sarah had passed, before following her into the front room.

And now Lizzie gathered up an armful of dishes and went into the scullery; a minute later the door clicked shut, and Corny and Mary Ann were alone together. Mary Ann stood with her back to him, a stiff, defiant, angry back, and she almost thought it was her da speaking when Corny's voice came at her, saying too quietly, 'You've got to make up your mind, and soon, if it's me you want or a big house and a lush life, because I can tell you here and now it'll have to be one or the other for a good many years because I can't see me getting rich quick, I'm not built that way. If I was I would have jumped at his offer and become a yes man, and I would have risen to manager, but the business would never have been mine. ... Oh, aye. ...' Although Mary Ann wasn't looking at him she knew he was wagging his head in wide sweeps. 'Oh, I know I was to be given a share, enough to enable me wife to live as he thinks she should live, as she would have lived if she had married Tony. ...' She swung round on him now but she didn't get a chance to speak, for his look stilled her tongue. Slowly he turned his gaze from her, and, picking up his cap from the chair, he went towards the scullery door, saying, still quietly, 'There it is. I'll give you time to think it over one way or the other. I'm going home now, but tell Michael I'll be back in the morning in plenty of time.'

As the door closed on him she put out her hand towards it, but she didn't move from where she was. Then, as if her legs had suddenly become tired with running, she found she had to sit down. She didn't want to cry; nor was she in a temper any longer; but filling her small body now was a feeling of fear. It said to her, 'You'd better go careful, you could lose him. You can't please both of them. And if you lose him you'll never get anybody to love you as he does, for in a way he loves you like your da does.' This was true, she knew, and

49

the ingredients in her love for him were similar to those in her love for her father. She had loved Corny from when he was a gangling boy, but she loved him more deeply when she recognized traits in him similar to those in Mike. She had a desire now to fly after him, and fling her arms about him, and cry, 'Corny ... Corny, have it any way you like, your way will suit me.'

At this moment Lizzie re-entered the kitchen. She did not look at Mary Ann as she gathered up the remainder of the dishes, but just as she was about to return to the scullery she said, 'He said he told you you've got to think about what you want, he's going to give you time.'

Mary Ann, looking up into Lizzie's face, knew that deep down in her, her mother would be glad if Corny and she were to break up. 'I won't need any time, I've done all the thinking I'm going to,' she said under her breath.

Lizzie paused as she was turning from the table, and her eyes asked, 'Well, and what are you going to do?'

'Whatever he wants will suit me in the long run.'

Lizzie did not immediately turn away, and when she did she sighed, and her lids drooped, and as she crossed the kitchen she remarked, as if to herself, 'That's the way it always works out.'

CHAPTER THREE

TAKING up the two front pews at the left-hand side of the church were Sarah's people – her aunts, her uncles, her cousins, but dominating them, the figure of her mother. Mrs. Flanagan was seated near the aisle. Her back was straight, her head was high; her thin face – which, to use Mrs. McBride's description, was snipy – was at this moment aglow with satisfaction. God was just. She had demanded that He would be so to her, for hadn't she struggled all her life against the environment of Burton Street, and what help had she got? . . . for he – meaning her husband – had done nothing in his life but disappoint her. And then for her only child to be afflicted with polio; she had thought that would be the end. But God's ways were strange; He had used the affliction as an instrument, and He had given her daughter courage to fight, and this had not gone unnoticed by Mr. Lord. Mrs. Flanagan did not think of Michael at this moment. Michael was just another one of God's instruments placed in Sarah's path to bring her to the notice of the influential owner of a shipping firm, a dock – even if it was only a small one – a farm, and a splendid house. Mary Ann Shaughnessy was not now alone the recipient of all good things.

The thought of Mary Ann brought Mrs. Flanagan's eyes to where Mary Ann herself was kneeling behind the bride and bridegroom, and if Mrs. Flanagan had ever given way to the weakness of gratitude she did so now, for she was thankful, she told herself, that Mary Ann had decided against making this a double wedding, for this was her daughter's day . . . and her own day, the day she would shine as the mother of the bride, the beautiful bride, for her daughter did look beautiful in spite of everything; but it would have been difficult to shine if she had been one of the mothers of the brides, the other mother being Lizzie Shaughnessy. Yes ... yes, she was grateful to Mary Ann for this.

At the other side of the aisle there sat in stronger force the friends and relations of the bridegroom, and Lizzie Shaughnessy was thinking much the same thing. Oh, she was glad that Mary Ann had decided against a double wedding, for with her heart so sore the strain of Mary Ann going at this particular time would have been too much – Mary Ann, she knew, was on her side, wholly and completely. The thought in itself was of some comfort, for she was a good ally to have, was Mary Ann; that was why, she supposed, she had at times been jealous of her whole-hearted affection for her da. At this point Lizzie became conscious of Mike standing by her side, almost touching her, yet they were poles apart; all that closeness that had been between them was gone, never to return. Nothing would ever be the same again. She wondered what he was thinking as he watched his only son being married. Was he remembering his own wedding day and the starvation years that followed, she wondered.

Mike wasn't remembering his own wedding day, or the starvation years that followed, but as he stared at the straight back of his son he thought, It'll pass him by, the torment, the hell; he'll hold to her through life, and if his love ever fades there'll be compassion. But he doubted if his love would fade. Sarah had a habit of working at things; because of her handicap she would work at marriage, not just accept it. No, there was no need to worry about that pair. And they were starting off well, with a fine little house, and Michael with a sure job ahead of him for the rest of his life. And what was more, people all around him were kindly and sympathetic to them both. ... And what had he himself started with? Kindness and sympathy? No. Censure all his life; from his upbringing in the cottage home which was part of the workhouse, until he met Liz. Then there were a couple of golden years, poor but golden, and although the gold dimmed as time went on it had never really tarnished, until these last few weeks. Mike's head moved downwards and his glance took in the black-gloved hand of his mother-in-law and the thought that took the feeling of guilt away was, And that's another thing Michael won't be handicapped with, an old fiend like this. He'll manage Mrs. F., but the devil in hell couldn't cope with this one. His head was immediately brought up by yet another thought: God in Heaven! What if she gets wind of this? He took his handkerchief and wiped the sweat away from around his face.

He's sweating, Mrs. McMullen commented to herself, and he's a right to, it's his sins oozing out of him. He's got a nerve to put his face in the church door. There should be some law about Protestants being allowed in the church; they should be made to sit separate like. She looked towards the altar. She wished the priest would put a move on, he was talking too much. They would find out what it was all about before long, especially her grandson. That poor lad had taken on a packet, he must be mad. If she had had anything to say in the matter it would never have come about . . . a cripple like her. Well, God worked in strange ways. There had been that talk of them going off on a holiday together, hadn't there, when they weren't even engaged; and people knew what happened on holidays. Well, Sarah Flanagan had paid in advance for that sinful thinking. . . . Aw, would the priest never finish? She was dying for a cup of tea and a drop of something in it – her legs were playing her up, like cramp she had, from the back of her heels up to her buttocks. . . . Aw, there they were coming from the altar, and not afore time. It was a disgrace it was, dressed in white and walking like that, like some drunk. It was a wonder Michael wasn't ashamed to be seen with her. Aye, she supposed, her face was all right, but that didn't make up for that dot-and-carry-one gait of hers. . . . Aw, and look at those two behind, the long and the short of it. Well, we get what we deserve, God sees to that. And she's going to get Fanny McBride's grandson, and good luck to her, she deserves no better. But of the two it's him that should be pitied, for if ever there was a little upstart it's that one. Look at her now walking down there as pious-looking as a saint, and mealy-mouthed into the bargain. If ever there was a creature with a mask on it's her. The damned little spitfire. Well, he's big enough, and I hope begod he takes it out of her. . . . And look at Old Flanagan there, grinning like a Cheshire cat. He's no man is that one,

53

as soft as clarts. . . . And now there was the big fellow, Mike himself, leaving her side and the pew and not giving her a hand up. Aw, well, his day would come, and it wasn't very far ahead if all rumours were right. For years she had told her daughter what he was, and what thanks had she got? Told to mind her own business. Well, it was her business. She pulled herself to her feet . . . she couldn't wait to get back to the house to get on with that particular business. There was never smoke without fire, and, as she said to herself as she walked up the aisle amid the crowd leaving the church, If I can bring a glow to the fire that's under him, God guide me.

Sarah was ready to go. She sat in the front-room dressed in a smart grey costume and a cherry-coloured hat. She looked quiet and utterly happy, and as Mary Ann stood holding her hand within her own two, she said softly, 'You look so serene.'

'I feel it . . . as if I was sort of filled with wonder.'

'Oh, I wish I was like you, Sarah.'

On this they both laughed, and Sarah said, 'Fancy saying that. Remember the fights, the rows? But it seems to me now as if they never happened, or they happened in a different life. You know what I mean?'

Mary Ann nodded her head. 'I wish you all the happiness in the world, Sarah; you know that, don't you?'

'Yes, Mary Ann.'

'And you know, Sarah?' Mary Ann squeezed her hand. 'I can say this to you now. You know, I've been a bit green about you, and I still am, because . . . well, I can see you going down the years supremely happy, no skull and hair flying between you and Michael, whereas us—' she spread out her free hand significantly, 'we're like two wild animals at times. You see, even today, on this very special day, we're not speaking.' She smiled wistfully. And Sarah could not help but laugh, as she replied, 'Well, you know something . . . as confessions seem the order of the day I might as well tell you that I'm not such a reformed individual as you think, for I've done my share of turning green. While you've been envying Michael and me for our placidness, for that's what

54

it really is, well, I've been jealous of you and Corny many a time when you've been going at one another.'

'What!'

'It's a fact. You see, you're both so boisterous, so full of life. That's how it should be when you're young. For myself, I feel I've been pushed into something that I shouldn't have realized for years and years, some kind of acceptance that only comes with age, if you know what I mean.'

'Aw, Sarah, don't think like that. Aw, you've been wonderful, wonderful. But' – she pulled a long face – 'I'm glad you've been jealous of me, it's a sort of comfort in a way. ...'

They were both laughing again, loudly now, their two heads together. They were like this when Lizzie found them, and she paused for a moment in the doorway before saying, 'Come on, come on, stop your carry-on the pair of you, everybody's waiting. They've all gone to the barn.'

Lizzie bustled around, gathering up Sarah's handbag, her case, her silk scarf, talking all the while to cover her feelings, to cover the fact that at this moment her son was leaving her for ever. There was no real thought for Sarah in her mind now, no affection; what was filling her mind and body was an agony that cried, Oh, Michael! ... Michael! She had lost her husband – she felt sure of this – and she was losing her son; in a different way perhaps, but more irrevocably, she was losing her son.

'Come on, come on.' She bustled them into the hall and to Michael, where he was standing waiting for his wife, and out of the front door and down the garden path towards the car and the crowd outside the barn.

Amid the confusion and good-byes, Michael now detached himself for a moment and, going to Mary Ann, to her utter surprise, he took her face between his hands and shyly kissed her, saying hastily, 'It's been fun knowing you.'

It was too much. Before the car was out of sight she was back in the front-room, standing with her face to the wall, very much as she had done when a child, and as she had often said when standing in such a position, Oh, our Michael! our Michael! She said his name again, but in a different way. He had said, 'It's been fun knowing you.' He had said that ... their Michael. Oh, our Michael! Our Michael!

'What's the matter with you?' Lizzie had come quietly into the room. She had not expected to see Mary Ann there.

'Oh, nothing. I just feel I've lost our Michael.'

'You feel you've lost our Michael?' Lizzie closed her eyes and, biting on her lip, hurried from the room.

It was eight o'clock and the jollification was going with a swing in the barn ... too much with a swing. There was too much noise, too much raucous laughter. Lizzie wished it was over. Oh God! How she wished it was over. To Lizzie's feelings now was added one of fear. She feared what she might do if she let herself go. For two solid hours she had watched that girl ogling Mike, she had watched them dance together. True it was in the lancers, and he had danced with others as well, but when he put his arm around her Lizzie felt it was with a difference. And there were others who were aware of it too. Her mother, hawk-eyed, waiting. She did not know how she hadn't sunk to the ground and dissolved in shame and tears as she watched them. That was until this feeling took possession of her, the feeling that urged her to get the girl outside, somewhere quiet, and thrash her with her hands, a stick, anything, anything.

Lizzie moved away from the barn doorway. Where was she now? She looked about her, her eyes searching the thronged floor. ... There she was. The bitch. Lizzie made no apology for the title. There she was dancing with Corny. ... But Corny didn't like her. Was he doing it to upset Mary Ann because of what happened yesterday? Oh! ... Like a gleam of light coming into the darkness of her mind came the thought, if only she would turn to Corny. Mary Ann was young; she would get over it; it was different when you were young. But now the gleam of light faded. This dance was the ladies' choice. It was she who had asked Corny. ... Then where was Mike? She remembered now that she hadn't seen him for quite some time.

'Ma.' Lizzie turned and looked at Mary Ann. In times of stress Mary Ann nearly always substituted ma for mother. 'Yes,' she said.

'Have you seen me da?'

Lizzie shook her head. 'No; why do you ask?'

'I haven't seen him for nearly an hour.'

'Have you looked?'

'Yes, in the house and all over.'

'Is the car in the garage?'

'Yes; I looked there.'

They stood close together now, their eyes scanning the room. 'Mrs. Radley's talking to me grannie,' said Mary Ann.

'I see that.'

'Ma.'

'Yes?'

They were still looking ahead.

'Me grannie's got wind of something.'

'How do you know?' The words came as a groan from Lizzie.

'She was at me, trying to stir me up, when they were dancing together. She caught hold of me as I was passing, and dug me in the ribs and said, "Look at that. How does that look to you, eh?"'

'What did you say?'

'I pretended I didn't know what she meant.'

'I . . . I don't think I can stand much more.' Lizzie's hand was encircling her throat and she strained her neck upwards as if she was choking.

'But, Ma' – Mary Ann caught hold of her arm and said softly and rapidly, 'You won't have to. He . . . promised me yesterday it's going to be over the night.'

Lizzie's eyes darted to Mary Ann's. 'What did he say?'

'Only that . . . that it'll be finished the night.'

Lizzie now moved her head in a bewildered way, and as Mary Ann was about to say something further there was a fuddled movement in the doorway to the right of them, a gurgle of a laugh, deep and well remembered, and they both swung round to see Mike smiling at them, and to see him as drunk as they had ever seen him for years.

'Oh, no, no.' Mary Ann put her hand to her mouth. She knew her da had disposed of a good many glasses since he returned from the church, but then he could stand a good many glasses both of beer and whisky. It took a lot to make him shake on his feet. Before she had time even to think anything further Mike had shambled the few steps towards them, and, gripping Lizzie roughly by the shoulder, he cried, 'Come on, Lizzie Shaughnessy, let's trip a measure. Come on.'

'Leave go of me.' Lizzie hissed the words at him. 'Stop it! Stop showing yourself up, and leave go of me.'

'Come on, it's a weddin', girl, it's a weddin'.'

Mary Ann watched her da reel and stumble almost on to his back as her mother thrust him forcibly from her. She knew that her da was what is termed rotten drunk, which meant fighting drunk. Anything could happen now. And after he had promised, promised faithfully to finish it. Oh. . . .

Mike was rocketing through the couples now, knocking them right and left with his swaying gait, causing laughter here, surprise there, and not a little uneasiness generally. And now he was thrusting Corny from Yvonne. Gripping her round the waist, he swung her into a staggering quick step. The next moment the inevitable had happened: they were both on the floor, as were the next two couples. Again the laughter was high, but only in some quarters.

When they got Yvonne to her feet her face was white. It could have been with shock or with anger, but no one was to know, for her mother quickly took charge and, guiding her to a seat, consoled her, while Mike lay with his legs spread-eagled and his one arm flaying the air.

As Lizzie rushed from the barn into the night Mary Ann followed her, but more slowly. It was the first time that she had turned from her da when he was in drink. Before, this fact had always drew her irresistibly to him to protect him from people's censure, and always the following morning from what was even worse, censure of himself.

As she saw the pale blur of her mother running towards the road, making for the house, she stopped; she couldn't follow her, she couldn't witness her pain. She stood with her knuckles pressed tightly to her teeth and her feelings in this moment took her beyond tears . . . she felt ashamed, degraded.

The door of the barn was wrenched open and Corny came running, making for the house. And then he saw her. Last night was forgotten. Immediately he put his arms about her and pressed her head gently to his shoulder, and they stood silent for some minutes, until Mary Ann's voice, in almost a whimper, said, 'Oh, Corny, how could he do it? And he promised to finish with her the night. He promised faithfully. He said it would be all over the night, and just look at him. . . .'

'What did you say about him finishing it?' Corny was now holding her from him, peering down into her face. 'He told you he was going to finish it?'

'Yes, he promised faithfully.'

'Well then.' His voice was high and his grip tightened on her shoulders and her body jerked under the movement of his hand. 'Don't you see? This is how he's doing it . . . getting blind drunk to put her off, to . . . well, to show her his other side as it were. . . . Can't you see?'

Mary Ann brought her eyes from the dim outline of Corny's face to the door of the barn. Then she whispered, 'You think that's why he's doing it?'

'Certain, because I've never seen him as blotto as this, and you know I've seen him when he's been pretty far gone and razing Burton Street.'

'Perhaps you're right. Now I come to think of it you are. . . . Oh, let's get him out.' She tugged at his arm now.

'Oh no, leave him to it – for a time, anyway. Let's walk quietly round the buildings.'

'But what if he's still carrying on when Tony and Lettice come back?'

'Well, they'll understand. But the old man . . . it's him I'll be worrying about . . . I wouldn't have him upset for anything, you know that.'

Although she couldn't see his face she knew from the tone of his voice that he was grinning at her, and she said softly, 'You. . . . Oh, Corny.' Then she added, 'About yesterday, you're right, I know you're right.'

Again he had his arms around her and again they were silent, until a great whoop of drunken laughter came from the barn and tore them apart, and Mary Ann cried, 'I've got to get him out, Corny.' And as she turned to go towards the door she stopped and, looking up at the dim figure at her side, exclaimed, almost in horror, 'Me grannie's in there. Aw, dear Lord, she only needed this to set her up for the rest of her life. Now he'll never live this down, never.'

When they opened the barn door there were no dancers on the floor, the band was having a rest and being entertained by the sight of the big one-armed red-headed bloke making a pass at a young girl in the corner.

Mike's antics had drawn the attention of the whole room towards him. He had his arm around Yvonne's shoulders and he was slobbering and grimacing and yammering as only a drunken man can. Mary Ann's eyes jerked to where her grannie was sitting. Her eyes riveted on her son-in-law, she looked like a female god, a self-satisfied female god. It was as if all her prophecies were being enacted before her eyes, and not only her own eyes but also of a large audience.

Mary Ann groaned audibly and was about to make her way across the room when Corny's hand gently stayed her, and he whispered down to her, 'Hold on a tick, just a minute or so.'

It was at this moment that Mr. Flanagan, self-appointed M.C., declared that they would now give the young-uns a chance to show their capers and have a twist.

As the band struck up Mike pulled himself to his feet with the obvious intention that Yvonne should partner him in the twist, but apparently the proceedings were becoming too much for Miss Radley's nerves, for now and in no gentle manner she tore her hand from his, pushed him upwards away from her to allow herself to rise, and as he reeled to the side she hurried as quickly as her stilt heels could carry her around the outskirts of the dancers and made for the door, there to be joined by her flurried mother and to be confronted by Mary Ann.

'You going?' As Mary Ann, with a great effort, forced an ordinary inquiring lightness into her tone, Yvonne Radley looked down at this interfering, tonguey little upstart, as she thought of her and she had the desire to take her hand and slap her mouth for her. She cast her glance towards Corny and her instinct told her that here was the one she would have gone after if he'd had any prospects, her mother or no mother. As if her mother had heard her thinking and decided right away to make clear their future policy she listened to her voice saying to Mary Ann with that calmness she both envied and hated, 'Well, we'll be going now, but we'll look in tomorrow perhaps.' There followed a pause before she added, 'Your father's in high fettle, isn't he, but that always happens at weddings. The soberest of men always let go at weddings, don't you think?'

Before Mary Ann could answer, 'But me da's not a sober man at any time,' Mrs. Radley put in quickly, 'Well come on, dear, we'll just go to the house and get our things . . . and say good-bye to your mother.' She nodded at Mary Ann, her long thin face and granite jaw pushed into a smile. 'She'll be glad when it's over, weddings mean nothing but hard work. Good night. We'll be seeing you soon.'

When the door closed on them, Mary Ann looked sadly up at Corny. 'It didn't work, they'll be back.'

'No, they won't; that was a face-saver.' He nodded quickly down at her. 'You'll see. As your da said he was going to, he's put an end to it.'

'You think so?'

'Sure of it. Come on, let's go out.'

'No. Look.' She made a small movement with her hand.

Mike was no longer standing where the Radleys had left him. He was now, to Mary Ann's horror, confronting her grannie. Swaying before her, he was telling her exactly how she was feeling.

'Bustin', aren't you? Bustin' at the seams with righteousness. Haven't . . . haven't you told Liz all these years what to expect, eh? An' haven't your words come true? Aye, an' with interest. You're gloatin', aren't you? Your black beady li'l eyes are full of divilish de-light. . . . Will I help you up now an' . . . an' push your creakin' bones over to Liz so's you can tell her once again how right you are . . . 'He's no good. Aa've told you afore an' Aa tell you now.' Come on, you rat-faced old divil; come on, an' I'll help you on your way, an' you can tell her. . . .'

'Da! Da!' Mary Ann was pulling on his arm, with Corny

at his other side, saying, 'Mike. Mike, come on, man ...
come on away.'

'Aw.' Mike was allowing himself to be turned from the
unblinking eyes and tight-lipped face of his mother-in-law
when Mrs. McMullen spoke. Addressing herself solely to
Mary Ann now, she said, 'You should feel at home now
you've got your old job back again. And it looks as if it might
be permanent. ...'

Mike almost swung Mary Ann off her feet, so quickly did
he jerk around, but Corny's bulk and young strength re-
strained him from returning to the attack, perhaps now with
more than words.

On their erratic journey towards the door they passed
Mrs. Flanagan. Her look held a mixture of disdain, patron-
izing pity, and self-glorification, and the glorification
covered her family. But she made no comment. Perhaps because Mr. Flanagan was standing close to her side, his hand
hidden in the fold of her dress. Mr. Flanagan was no longer
the worm that she had created in the early years of her
marriage. Mr. Flanagan was now a person to be contended
with, so much so that when he nipped her leg she did not
even turn on him, she just kept her mouth shut.

They were outside when Mike, jerking his body from
right to left, freed himself from their clutching hands and
cried loudly, and angrily, 'Leave over, leave me go, I'm not a
child you're playin' with, I'm a man an' I make me own
decisions. Do you hear that?' He was leaning towards Mary
Ann, peering at the outline of her that seemed to have grown
even smaller. 'I do things in me own way. You see. Well, it's
over. I promised you, didn't I? But in my own way, I said,
an' with no words. ... No, begod! No words on ... on either
side, 'cos you can't end with words somethin' that's never
been started with words, can you now?'

As Mary Ann gazed unseeing up at Mike and felt the gust
of his breath fall on her she realized that, although he was
drunk, he wasn't half as drunk as he had made out to be in
the barn.

'Well now, back to normal, eh? Back to normal and everybody happy. Aw God, yes, everybody happy.' There was
such sadness in his tone now that she wanted to fling her

arms around him and comfort him, but he was moving away, and although he was still swaying his step was much steadier than it had been.

When Mary Ann heard the little wicket gate bang shut, she knew that he had not gone to the house but into the fields. And as she felt Corny's hand groping for hers, she said sadly, 'Let's go to me ma.'

Lizzie was in the kitchen. She had been standing looking down at the fire, but she turned her head swiftly as they entered the room.

Mary Ann went to her side while Corny stood at the table.

'They came over for their clothes. Have they gone?'

Lizzie made no answer but turned her eyes towards the fire again.

'Ma.' Mary Ann was clasping Lizzie's arm with her two hands. 'Sit down for a minute. Come on, sit down, I've got something to tell you.'

'I don't want to hear anything more.' Lizzie's head drooped, yet she turned from the fire and sat down on the chair that Corny brought forward. Then raising her weary face to Mary Ann, who was now standing in front of her, she said, 'Where is he?'

'Outside.'

'Going to take them home in his condition?' Her voice was bitter.

'No, Ma, no.' Mary Ann shook her head. 'He's gone into the fields. Ma—' she stood close beside her mother, holding her hand tightly, 'he did it on purpose, it was his way of breaking it off, to show her ... well, what he was like – in drink I mean ... you see?'

Lizzie saw, and she lowered her head. Then raising it again she looked at Corny and, asking for confirmation, said, 'You really think so?'

It was as he nodded that Mary Ann put in, 'It was Corny who realized it first. He saw why he was doing it, and I know now it's true, because knowing how our Michael hated me da when in drink he would have done anything rather than get drunk the day. You can see that, can't you? ...' Mary Ann now lifted Lizzie's hand up towards her breast and asked pleadingly, 'Be nice to him. Talk to him, he'll feel awful the morrow . . . will you?'

'I'll see . . .' said Lizzie slowly. Then sighing, she added, 'Your grannie'll be here until tomorrow night. After that perhaps . . . perhaps things might get back to normal. . . . They might.'

'I've always wished she'd never set foot in the house, but tonight, of all nights, I wish it. And he's been for her already.'

'What! In the barn?' Lizzie's tone was sharp.

'Yes.'

'I'd better go over. You're sure he's not there?'

'No, Ma, no; he went through the bottom gate.'

As Lizzie moved across the room, she said, 'The electric blanket's on in the front-room bed—' She no longer called it Sarah's bed. 'Will you see to the bottles for upstairs?'

'All right, Ma, I'll see to them.'

When they were alone together, Corny sat down in Mike's chair to the side of the fireplace and, holding out his hand, said softly, 'Come here.'

When Mary Ann went to him he lifted her as lightly as if she had been a child and sat her on his knee, and, looking at her, he said briefly, 'Let's make our day as soon as possible, eh?'

'Our wedding? . . . But . . . but we said December.'

'I know, but there's no need to wait that long, the date wasn't fixed. We could do it in November, say about the middle.'

She waited a moment; then moving her head slowly, she said, 'All right. I'll . . . I'll go and see Father Owen and make arrangements for us to see him together. Will I?'

'Yes . . . yes, do that.'

His arms slid over one another as they pressed her to him, and she lay against him, not joyful but sad and quiet; and when his voice, close to her ear, said, 'We'll make a big go of it, us two together; we'll show 'em how it really should be done,' she turned her face into the opening of his coat and began to cry.

CHAPTER FOUR

'IT's not right for an old woman to be on her own. I could be taken ill or drop down dead and who would know but God himself.' Mrs. McMullen shook her abundantly haired head at the sadness of it all. 'I'd be in nobody's way in the front-room there. If you could put up with strangers for two years, and after all what was Sarah but a stranger to you, then you should consider the nearest of your kith and kin, and who's nearer your kith and kin than your own mother?'

'I want my front-room for myself.' Lizzie was mixing a batter as she stood at the long table, her gaze concentrated on her moving hand.

'I've never heard anything so selfish in my life.'

'Perhaps not.'

'I'm nearing eighty.'

'I'm aware of that.'

There followed a pause, and it added significance and emphasis to Mrs. McMullen's next words. 'Aw, well, you never know but that you'll be offering it to me in a very short time. With them all gone and you on your own you might be glad of company.'

As Lizzie's hands became still Mary Ann came in from the hall. Her face looked small and pinched, and she glared at her grannie as she cried, 'The day me ma'll be entirely on her own won't matter to you very much because you'll be dead.'

'Mary Ann!' Lizzie turned sharply towards her.

'Nice, isn't it?' Mrs. McMullen's head dropped downwards as she spoke. 'All ready to go to mass she is and she comes out with things like that. If any girl has taken advantage of her convent education I would say it was your daughter, Lizzie.'

'Aw, I don't care what you say about me, Grannie, you've never said a good word about me in your life and I don't expect you to start now, but let me tell you. . . .' As Mary Ann advanced across the room, Mrs. McMullen brought her head up sharply to meet the onslaught. 'The only way me mother would be left alone is if you come to live here. And the Lord himself knows, when that happens—'

'Mary Ann!' Lizzie had her daughter by the shoulders now, and, swinging her about, propelled her forcibly back towards the hall, and when she had her there she pushed the kitchen door closed with her foot, saying under her breath, 'As she said, you're going to mass and this is no way to—'

'Look, Ma, the old devil won't rest until she's in that room.' Mary Ann thumbed violently towards the front-room door. 'And if you want to drive me da away you let that happen.'

'She's not coming here, now or at any other time.'

'Honest?'

'Honest.' Lizzie closed her eyes. 'Don't you think I've had enough to put up with without asking for more. Be sensible, girl.'

'Yes, yes, I know.' Mary Ann took in a deep breath, then added, 'But I also know her. She'll keep on till she wears you—'

'She won't wear me down, never.'

'But what would happen if, as she says, she took bad?'

'Then she'll go to hospital, or I'd travel all the way down to Shields every day to see to her, but I won't let her come here.'

Mary Ann's tight gaze dropped from Lizzie's; then her head sank down towards her chest as she asked, quietly, 'Have . . . have you spoken to me da?'

Her mother's silence brought her head up again, and when their eyes met they held for a moment before Lizzie answered, 'It'll take a little time, but don't worry.' She put out her hand and touched Mary Ann's arm gently with her finger. 'It'll come all right now, so don't worry any more.'

'And you'll stop worrying?'

'Yes . . . yes.' Lizzie sighed. 'It takes two to make a quarrel and two to mend it, you understand?'

'Yes, Mother.'

'Go on, get yourself off or you'll miss the bus.'

Before Mary Ann turned away she asked, 'Can I bring Corny back to dinner?'

'Yes, of course. ... But I thought he went to Mrs. McBride's?'

'Not every Sunday, he sometimes has it at home.'

'Well, please yourself; he's welcome, as you know.'

When Lizzie closed the door on Mary Ann she stood with her back to it for a few minutes, as if fortifying herself before returning to the kitchen.

As she entered the room she saw that her mother was sitting stiff and straight in her chair, with her index finger tapping out a slow rhythm on the wooden arm; this was always a bad sign. Lizzie picked up the bowl of batter, went into the scullery and put it in the fridge; then, returning to the kitchen, she was in the act of clearing a small side-table when her mother said, 'How long has it been going on?'

Again Lizzie's hands became still, before she answered, 'What do you mean?'

'Now, don't try to pull the wool over my eyes, because even if you did I could still see, I'm not blind. If he had humiliated me as he's done you I would send him flying. A young piece like that! Brash as they come. But he picked his own colour ... like to like.'

'Be quiet!' Lizzie had swung round from the table but was pressing her hips into its edge, and she stood twisting her hands as if aiming to wrench them from the wrists, as she cried, 'There's nothing in it, nothing, I tell you. It's in your mind, your bad mind. You would like it to happen, wouldn't you? You've been waiting for it for years. Well, I tell you it won't happen, it's finished. ... It never started, it was nothing. ... And I should know, who better? If I was worried about it I would have done something about it, wouldn't I? Well, I've done nothing, not lifted a finger. That's just how much I was worried. Some girls are all mixed up inside and this causes them to make a dead set at older men, but it doesn't say that the older man makes anything of it other than something to laugh at, and that's how it is. For your information, that's how it is.' She bent her

67

body from the table while still keeping her buttocks pressed against it. 'That's what happened in this case, so make out of it what you like.'

As her mother and she exchanged glances, one sceptical, the other defiant, Lizzie became aware of a movement in the scullery. She had been shouting so hard, she hadn't heard anyone come in, but as she turned away from her mother she saw from the window who it was who was going quietly out. Mike was making his exit towards the back gate, not on the paved path, but on the grass verge. Lizzie pressed her lips tightly together and her face puckered painfully. How much had he heard? Enough, she supposed, to make him creep out like that. The breath that she took into her body lifted her breasts upwards. Well, as she had said to Mary Ann, it took two to mend a quarrel. She had done her part, now the rest was up to him. He knew where he stood with her, and now she could await his reaction.

The almost silent dinner was drawing to a close when the front door bell rang. Lizzie raised her head, Mary Ann raised her head, Mrs. McMullen went on scraping the remains of her pudding from her plate, and Corny, rising from the table, said, 'I'm nearest, I'll see who it is.'

Mike pushed his chair back and went to the fireplace and took his pipe from the mantelpiece. He was standing with his back to the fire, scraping the bowl, when the muffled but recognizable voices came to him, and he stared, or rather gaped, towards the door to where Corny was standing aside to allow Mrs. Radley and her daughter to enter the room.

'We were on our way to Newcastle to my cousin's for tea, but we thought we could drop in to see how you're all faring after the excitement of yesterday.'

Lizzie, her eyes wide, her mouth tight, stared at the woman. Then her gaze slowly moved to Yvonne, but the girl was not looking at her; she was looking across the room at Mike, and her brown eyes soft and moist were forgiving him for his misdemeanour of last night. Lizzie's head now moved to take in her husband's face. There was a white line around his mouth, standing out against the ruggedness of his weather-beaten complexion, and there was a look on his face she had never seen before. She likened it to that of a ship-wrecked man who, sighting the shore, felt the tide turning beneath him and knew that he was helpless against it. Deep from within her there arose the familiar prayer, but in the form of a cry, 'Holy Mary, Mother of God, pray for us sinners now and at the hour of our death!'

CHAPTER FIVE

'It's good of you to see me, Father.'

'It's good to see you, Mary Ann.' The priest put out his hand tentatively and touched her cheek. 'You're looking a bit pale. Are you all right?'

'Yes, Father.'

'And everybody at home?'

'Yes, Father.'

'Ah, sit down, Mary Ann, and let's have a crack. . . . It's a long time since we had a wee crack, isn't it?' The priest lent his long length towards her, and she smiled widely at him. Oh, Father Owen was nice, wasn't he? Comforting; like Mrs. McBride in a way, only different. She had always been able to talk to these two people without reserve. Well, not quite without reserve to Father Owen. Whereas she could openly discuss her da's weakness with Mrs. McBride, she had already tried to hide it from the priest. Not that her efforts accomplished anything in the long run, for he always got to the bottom of things.

'It was a lovely wedding, Sarah and Michael's, wasn't it?'

'Yes, Father, lovely.'

'They should be very happy. . . . Have you seen them since?'

'Yes, Father. They both came over on Monday night . . . they made on they felt lonely.' She laughed. 'Michael said he missed the farm, and Sarah said she missed the house and me ma and me, but nobody believed them.'

'And I don't blame them.' They were both laughing now. 'And if I know anything, Sarah will be at the farm as much as Michael when he gets back to work. That car is a godsend. . . . You know, Mr. Lord is a very good man, Mary Ann.'

'I know that, Father.' She nodded at him. 'I can't imagine

70

where we would have been without him. But yes I can . . . still in Burton Street.'

'Yes, perhaps . . . perhaps you're right, Mary Ann.' The priest paused. Then putting his head on one side, he went on, 'He's an old man, set in his ways, and the only pleasure he's got in his life is doing little things for other people. Of course, it all depends on what you call little. But he likes to help, Mary Ann, you know that?'

'Yes, Father.' She sat stiffly now, knowing what was coming.

'His intentions are always good, I'm sure of that, no matter how things appear, and you know, Mary Ann, I think it's very foolish of Corny to have turned down his offer.'

Mary Ann did not ask the priest how this piece of news had come to his knowledge. Years ago she had likened Father Owen to God, and the impression at times still held. She looked straight at him as she said, 'It's no use, Father, he won't be persuaded; he's got his own ideas about what he wants to do . . . and . . . and I'm going along with him.'

The priest's head went back now and he let out a high laugh. 'Aw, it's funny it is to hear you say you're going along with anybody, Mary Ann. The individualist of individualists following a leader. Aw, well, perhaps it's a good thing.'

After her laughter had died down, the priest waited a moment, giving her the chance to state the reason for her visit, but when she sat looking at her hands he prompted gently, 'and what were you wanting to see me about, Mary Ann?'

She raised her eyes to his without lifting her head. 'We . . . we wanted to bring our wedding forward, Father. We . . . we thought about the beginning of November instead of December.'

Father Owen stared at her, and although his eyes didn't leave her face, Mary Ann knew that he was seeing her as a whole, and the thought this prompted brought a rush of blood to her face and caused her to bring out in fluttering protest, 'No, Father . . . no, there's no reason, Father. I mean we just want to get married sooner.'

She watched the shadow pass from the priest's face and his eyes light up, and the lightness came over in his voice as he cried, 'And why not? Why not indeed!' Mary Ann did not return his smile but said soberly, 'You were going to see us one or two evenings before. . . .'

'Yes, yes, that can be arranged at any time. . . . Tell me, have you discussed the future between yourselves?'

'Yes, Father; yes, a bit.'

'You've talked about children?'

'Yes, Father.'

'And you yourself want children, Mary Ann . . . sincerely want them?'

'Oh, yes, Father, yes.' Now she did smile at him, her eyes and mouth stretching with the achievement she would in time accomplish. 'I'm going to have three, Father,' she said; 'two girls and a boy.'

'Oh?' The priest's long face took on a comic serious expression. His eyebrows formed points directed towards his white hair, and his voice was flat as he said, 'Three?' Then again 'Three! You've got it all cut and dried, Mary Ann, like the rest of them. Tell me, why stop at three? That is, if the good God means you have any at all. But if He does, I ask you, why stop at three? . . . You know something?' He bent towards her again and poked out his long turkey neck as he stated firmly, 'I'm one of thirteen.'

'You are, Father? Thirteen!'

'Ah-ah. Ah-ah. Thirteen, and there wasn't a happier family living, although mind, it was a bit hectic at times.'

'Oh, you're poor mother!' Mary Ann shook her head, and her lips were now pressed together to stop her laughter.

'Aw, you needn't pity her, for she was in her element. It was her vocation to have children, and she reared every one of those thirteen children with the sole help of Hannah Anne.'

'Hannah Anne?'

'Yes, Hannah Anne.' The priest looked across at the sparsely furnished room to where, on the wall, hung a large portrait of Our Lady, and he seemed to be talking to the picture rather than to Mary Ann as he went on, 'Out of all the millions of impressions that a child takes in . . . that a youth takes in, only a few come over with him into manhood, only a few remain clear-cut, the rest are vague and have to be grabbed at and pulled into the light, but a few remain clear. . . . Hannah Anne remained clear.'

Mary Ann was no longer smiling, she was looking up at this old priest who she felt at this moment had gone from her; although he was talking to her, he was no longer with her, and she said no word, made no sound to prompt him onwards, but waited, and then he said, 'Mondays and Fridays, those are the days I always connect with Hannah Anne, Mondays and Fridays.' He turned his face now towards Mary Ann, but his eyes still looked unseeing as he went on, 'You see, she washed all day on Monday, and she baked all day on a Friday. She baked yuledoos on a Friday; you know what I mean, bits of dough with currants in. There were nine of us when she first came to the house, and she made nine separate yuledoos, all different sizes according to our ages. I was fourteen then and Hannah Anne fifteen. She was paid one and sixpence a week and she slept under the roof.' His head drooped slightly, and so quiet did he become that it almost seemed as if he was dozing. But Mary Ann knew he wasn't dozing. He was back in his boyhood standing in the kitchen waiting for his yuledoo from Hannah Anne, who was just a year older than himself. Then with a quick movement that almost startled her he was back with her again, and from the look on his face she knew that he was going to speak no more of Hannah Anne. But she wanted to hear more, so she said quickly, 'Did you lose sight of her, Father?'

'Lose sight of her?' There was surprise in his tone. 'No, no, she's in Felling to this day, and every time I'm that way I call.' He screwed up his face at her. 'I try to make it on a Friday for she still bakes on a Friday, but tea cakes now, and she's generous with the butter.' His chin moved outwards. 'No, Hannah Anne is still going strong. And you know something? She was twenty-seven when she married. She waited until we were all up, so to speak, and then she married, and I, Mary Ann . . . I performed the ceremony. It was my first wedding. People laugh, you know, when they hear of folks crying at weddings.' He had once again turned his eyes from her, and once again they were on the picture on the wall, and Mary Ann's heart became sore for something intangible, something that could not be spoken of, something that might have been if God had willed it; something between Hannah Anne who washed on a Monday and baked on a Friday and was just a year older than a boy of fourteen. Hannah Anne who had shown the priest how easy it was to cry at a wedding. Quite suddenly she decided to let God, and of course Corny, settle as to the size of her coming family. She put her thoughts into words by saying gently, 'I'll let things take their course, Father.'

'That's it, that's it, Mary Ann, let things take their course. It's a wise decision. Now when do I see you and Corny? Say on Tuesday evening at half past seven, how's that?'

'That will be fine, Father.'

She rose from the chair, and Father Owen, getting to his feet, said, 'Now will you have a cup of tea before you go? Miss Neilson always has the pot on the hob.'

'Thanks all the same, Father, but I've got to go to Mrs. McBride's; Corny's meeting me there.' She had no desire to meet the priest's housekeeper, for she still had memories of that gaunt lady's reception of her in the past.

'Aw, you're going to Fanny's. Well, give her my regards, although it's not over two days since I last saw her. She keeps fine, doesn't she? In spite of everything, she keeps fine.' He bent his long length down towards her and grinned as he said, 'She'll take some killing that one, what do you think?'

'I think like you, she'll take some killing, Father. And I'm glad.'

'That makes two of us.'

'Good-bye, Father.'

'Good-bye, Mary Ann. Don't forget, half past seven on Tuesday night the pair of you. God bless you. Good-bye now.'

She walked up the street, crossed the road in the direction of Burton Street, and as she went her mind reiterated: Thirteen children ... I don't think I'd want thirteen; it would wear you out, wouldn't it, thirteen. And they'd all have to be fed and clothed ... and if the garage didn't go all right ... Aw – she literally shook herself – what was she going on about? Thirteen children. ... But what if she did have ...?

Aw, she was mad, daft, thinking this way. As she had said to Father Owen, let things take their course.

In a few weeks she would be married. Her step became slower. She couldn't quite take it in, but she was glad they weren't waiting until December. When the true reason for this came to her she tried to turn away from it, to bang a door in her mind shut on it, but the fact still remained clear before her, she wanted to get away from home. She wanted to get away from the sight of her da. The da who had become weak, the da who had lost his power to create wonder in her. Nothing had apparently changed since the Radleys' visit last Sunday afternoon; an onlooker might imagine that Mike Shaughnessy had made his stand last Saturday night and was abiding by it, but she knew differently. She was too close to Mike not to gauge his feelings, and she knew that before him lay a course from which he was shying. She knew, and he knew, that the only way to treat this matter was with decisive action, to openly tell the pair of them not to come back to the house again. But she also knew that it was almost impossible for her da to take such action towards a girl who was being charming to him, for he wouldn't want to be confronted with the look of feigned incredulity and the consequent reply of, 'You've got ideas about yourself, haven't you? Fancy you thinking like that; why, you're old enough to be my father.' And Mary Ann knew that was the kind of retort he would get from a girl like Yvonne Radley once she was made aware that she was wasting her time, and he wasn't strong enough to face being made to look an old fool.

She should be happy and joyful because she was to be married – she loved Corny with all her heart – yet here she was, sad to the soul of her. For the first time in her life she felt dislike and bitterness well up in her against her da; and she said to herself, If he keeps it up I won't own him, I won't, I won't!

It was Sunday afternoon again and Lizzie had all her family around her. This, she knew, should have made her the happiest woman on earth: there was Michael and Sarah looking so radiant that it brought a soft pain to her heart;

there was Mary Ann, a quieter, more subdued Mary Ann these days, and Lizzie felt she liked her daughter better this way, she seemed more predictable. Yet one never knew with Mary Ann. And there was Corny, talking, talking, talking. She should be thankful for Corny, grateful to him, for she knew why he was talking. He was, in his own way, aiming to bring a lightness to the atmosphere, and she really was grateful to him. There were sides to Corny that she could not help but admire, sides that she could trace back to his grannie; one side, in particular, that made him wise . . . heart wise. . . . And then there was Mike. Her husband was sitting to the side of the fireplace, smoking. He might appear at ease, but she knew that, like herself, he was on tenterhooks, he was waiting. . . . If they had been on the two-o'clock bus they would have been here before now, but there was always the three-o'clock, and the four-o'clock. How many times, she wondered, had he seen her since last Sunday? During the past week he had been out only once in the evening, and then for not more than two hours. But a lot could happen in two hours. She had wanted to tackle him on his return and say 'Well?' but she had thought better of it, there might just be the chance that he hadn't been with her. Sometimes she told herself she was making a mountain out of a molehill, that there was nothing in it, only what her imagination put there. She explained the situation to herself; Mrs. Radley and her daughter were two people they had met at a holiday camp, wasn't it natural that they should pop in and see them now and again? But the answer that burst from her tortured mind was, 'Natural that they come every Sunday and her looking like that? Contriving always to expose herself in some way: showing off her bust with her low, square necklines; sitting with her legs crossed so that her skirt rode almost to her thighs.' No, she was no fool. That girl meant business . . . and her mother meant business. Once during the last few days she had said to herself, 'I'll walk out and leave him.' But then her reason told her that that was what they were waiting for. Like a double-headed cobra, they were waiting their time to strike. For a moment she saw them ensconced in her house, in her front-room, which, since Sarah's departure, had become 'her' room again.

Lizzie's mind was brought from herself by Corny speaking to her, and she turned to him and said, 'What was that, I didn't get what you said?'

'I was just sayin,' said Corny, 'that she should send this one to one of the magazines, the ones that sell round the North-East.'

'Which one is that?'

'The one called "The Northerner".'

'Oh, give over.' Mary Ann reached out to grab the sheet of paper from Corny's hand. 'Me mother hasn't heard it.'

'She hasn't?' Corny looked at Lizzie again. 'Well, it's about time she did,' he said. 'Listen to this.'

Lizzie listened as she looked at the big fellow, standing in a set pose, his arm extended as he read what was apparently Mary Ann's latest effort at poetry.

'The Northerner,' announced Corny in the grandiose manner:

> 'I longed for spring after winter gales,
> And sleet and snow and muddy feet,
> But when it came it quickly passed,
> And summer followed, and that was fleet.
> Then autumn brought me thoughts of wind,
> Of raging, tearing, swirling air.
> And, as a dreamer, I awoke
> To beauty of trees dark and bare,
> Of branches lashed with sleet and rain,
> Of racing cloud and raging sea,
> And I was bidden to rise and greet
> The winter which is part of me.'

'There now. Isn't it good?'

Sarah was the first to answer. 'I think it's grand,' she said; 'it says what it means.'

'Yes, it's quite good.' Michael pulled on his cigarette as he lay back in the corner of the couch; then with a brother's prerogative he added, 'But I think it's a bit too simple, I mean to get into a magazine or anything.'

'Simple, you say? Of course it's not too simple.' Corny was on the defensive. 'Anyway, that's how people want things written, so's that they can understand them.'

'There is simple and ... simple, old fellow. There's the simplicity of things like "Milk Wood" ...'

'Aw, you and "Milk Wood". We had this out afore, re-member?' Corny now threw himself into a chair opposite Michael. 'Because you went on about it, I read it. And you know what? It's snob stuff. He mightn't have meant it that way when he wrote it, but I'd like to bet me bottom dollar that seventy-five per cent of people who read it do so because they think it's the thing to do, sort of slumming in litera-ture. ...'

'Slumming! "Milk Wood"? Go on, man, you don't know what you're talking about.' Michael laughed derisively.

'Don't I?' Corny pulled himself to the edge of the chair, and he spread his glance over Mary Ann, Sarah, Lizzie and Mike, who were all sitting now like people waiting to be entertained, and he went on, 'I'm tellin' you: half the people that read that kind of stuff neither understand nor like it, but they're afraid to say that they don't because they'll be looked upon as unintelligent nitwits.'

'What do you know about it, Corny?' Michael was smiling with a quiet, superior smile now, a smile that was meant to draw Corny on still further. 'Have you joined a literary society or something?'

'No, I haven't, and I wouldn't if they paid me, but I read; I read what I like, not what they tell me to read in the reviews, 'cos what happens then? Some bloke quotes two lines of something out of a book and they sound wonderful and you break your bloomin' neck to go and get the book, and before you're half-way through the damn stuff you re-alize you're being had. All the fellow wrote in that book was those two lines, all the rest is what you or anybody else could think of. But some bloke, I mean a reviewer, for one of a dozen reasons picks on those two lines, and when you can't like the book you get the feeling there is something wrong with you up here.' He prodded his head with his forefinger. 'And you start to ask why.'

'Very good question, Corny, a very good question to ask yourself, and it's about time you did, too.'

'Give over, Michael, stop teasing.' Sarah pushed at her husband, and they both laughed and looked at Mary Ann.

And Mary Ann laughed, and Lizzie smiled faintly, but Mike ... he just kept looking at Corny, his countenance giving nothing away, not of amusement or interest, and Corny, going back into the attack, demanded of Michael, 'Come on, let's know what you've read. Have you read Steinbeck, John Steinbeck?'

'Oh, years ago.'

'What? What did you read of his?'

'Oh, I've forgotten.'

'If you had read Steinbeck, man, you wouldn't have forgotten a word of it. An' I bet you've never heard of Salinger, eh, have you?'

'Of course I've heard of him.'

'Have you read him? Have you read *The Catcher in the Rye*? ... No, you haven't. Well, it's a marvellous book. He's a marvellous writer ... an American.'

'You don't say!' Michael was now shaking with laugher and Corny, suddenly thrusting his hands out, gripped him by the collar and pulled him off the couch and on to the floor. At this Lizzie cried, 'Give over! Give over, the pair of you. Corny, get up. Michael, do you hear me? Stop acting like children.'

Still laughing, they broke apart, and Michael, taking his seat again beside Sarah, looked at her as he straightened his tie and remarked in a mock serious tone. 'Her a poetess and him a literary critic ... coo! Won't we have something to brag about? ... 'Cos neither of them can spell!'

'Now stop it, Corny!' Lizzie clamped down on yet another attack, and Corny, putting his coat to rights, cried, 'There's many a true word said in a joke.' He was now nodding his big head at Michael, and Michael, returning the same gesture, answered solemnly, 'True, true, Victor Ludorum of the literary field. True, true. Ah! How true.'

Corny, now screwing up his eyes questioningly, asked, 'Victor Lu ... who? Who's he? Never heard of him.'

'He was in a band, blew a cornet before he started ...'

'Stop it, our Michael!' Mary Ann thrust out her hand towards her brother. 'Don't be so clever.'

'Well, I'm only telling him.' Michael was shaking with laughter again.

'O.K., I'm willing to learn, who is he? I can't know them all, can I, and if you don't ask you never know.'

'You want your ears boxed, our Michael. Box his ears, Sarah.' Mary Ann was on her feet, and, thrusting out her hand and grabbing hold of Corny, said, 'Come on, I want to go for a walk.'

'But I want to get to the bottom. . . .'

Michael was now rolling helplessly on the couch, and he clutched at Sarah as he tried to speak, and Mary Ann cast a withering glance at him and cried again, 'Come on. Do you hear, Corny?'

Corny, grinning, and scratching his head with one hand, allowed himself to be tugged across the room, and as he passed Mike's chair Mike touched him on the sleeve, and, looking up into his face, said, with strange gentleness, 'You'll be Victor Ludorum in anything you take up; you'll master all that comes, Corny, never you fear.'

As they exchanged glances the grin slid from Corny's face. Then, still being led by Mary Ann, he went out into the hall and on into the kitchen, and there, pulling her to a stop, he said under his breath, 'What's this Victor Ludorum lark? Who is he, anyway?'

Mary Ann dropped her lids for a moment before looking up at him, saying, 'It's just a term, Corny. It's for whoever comes top of the sports at school, it's a Latin term meaning victor of the games.'

'Aah.' He stared at her for a long moment, and again he said, 'Aah.' Then, rubbing his hand across his wide mouth, he remarked, 'That's what comes of not going to a grammar school. . . . Still—' his eyebrows moved up, 'we live and learn, don't we?'

'Michael didn't mean anything, you know that. He wasn't trying to be clever or anything. It's just that he's so slap-happy he doesn't know what he's saying half the time.'

'Aw, I don't take any notice of Michael.' He turned from her and walked slowly down the length of the long kitchen, and as he went he muttered, 'Victor Ludorum. Your da says I'll be Victor Ludorum in anything I take up.' He turned his head slightly and glanced down at her. 'Victor of the games, you said; master of anything, Mike said. Well! Well!'

They went out through the scullery and down the garden path that led to the road, and although he had hold of her hand and they were walking close together, she knew that he wasn't with her. This silly business had put a bee in his bonnet. She almost felt it taking shape: Victor Ludorum ... Victor of the literary game! She wanted to go back and slap their Michael's face for him. Showing up Corny's ignorance like that. And yet ... and yet Corny wasn't ignorant. Corny had read more than their Michael, much more.

When he turned his head towards her and said abruptly, 'I am the captain of my soul, I am the master of my fate. It's the same thing, isn't it, as this Victor Ludorum?' she remained silent. It wasn't really; one was physical, the other was mental and spiritual. ... Or was it? Was conquering your fate physical? Oh, she didn't know, it was the kind of thing that took thinking out. But Corny was waiting for an answer and he wanted her to say, yes, it was the same thing, because he intended to be master of his fate, did Corny. And so she smiled softly as she replied, 'Yes, Corny, it's the same thing exactly.'

With a sudden jerk he pulled her hand up through his arm, and with a step to which she had to trot he marched her down the road.

Already, she knew, he was Victor Ludorum.

CHAPTER SIX

THE weeks that followed went with different speeds for different members of the family. For Lizzie, each day dragged, yet, overall, they seemed to move too fast and ominously towards Sundays, when the visitors would call, sometimes to stay only for an hour, sometimes to stay for as long as four or five. It all depended if they had to wait to see Mike or not. But if their visits were along or short, during them Lizzie tortured herself all the while as she watched for some signal, some look to pass between Mike and the girl which might mean the arranging of a meeting or a change of plan. Now he went out twice a week in the evenings, and with the coldness forming into ice between them, she could not break through and inquire, even in anger, where he'd spent his time.

For Mary Ann the days were moving too fast. It was only just over a fortnight before she would be married, and nothing settled yet about the garage. But perhaps Corny would clinch it this afternoon. She hoped so. Oh, she did, she did, because she didn't want to start her married life living at home. A few months ago she wouldn't have minded a jot, but not now.

She came down the stairs and into the kitchen, and Lizzie, turning and looking at her, said flatly, 'You're off then?'

'Yes, I'm meeting Corny at the garage; it might be settled this afternoon.'

'I hope so,' said Lizzie kindly.

'Thanks, Mother. ... You wouldn't like to come along with me? It's a nice day, the outing would do you good.'

'No, thanks, lass. Michael and Sarah might pop over and I wouldn't like to be out if they came.'

'All right.' She nodded. 'But don't wait tea for us, you never know how long it will take ... that's if the business gets going.'

'Will he move out straight away if it's settled?' asked Lizzie.

'He said he would ... he said he's going to live with his daughter. He's got nothing much left in the flat upstairs anyway, she's already seen to that ... the daughter I mean. ... Well, I'll be off.' She kissed Lizzie's cheek. 'Bye-bye, Mother.'

'Bye, bye, dear.' Lizzie now looked Mary Ann up and down before saying, 'I like you in that coat; that particular blue suits you and it adds to your height.'

Mary Ann leaned forward and again kissed Lizzie, then hurried out without making any comment. It hurt her when her mother was kind, because she knew the effort it must take to say nice things, feeling as she did, desolate and lost, and ... and spurned. Yes, that was the word, for her da was spurning her ma openly now.

As she went up the lane towards the main road she glanced about her. Her da would likely be walking the fields, she had heard him whistle Simon earlier on. Not that she wanted to see him; this looking for him was only a habit. As she rounded the bend of the lane she heard Simon bark, but she could not see the dog, or Mike. Likely they were in the old barn. She looked towards the building that stood somewhere off the road on the edge of a field path, and then her gaze darted to the further end of the lane to where two people were walking with their backs to her. They were Yvonne and Mrs. Radley. Her heart gave a double sickening beat and she thought bitterly, Oh, me da, having her here on the sly. It didn't lighten the accusation that the mother was with Yvonne. She was always with her; she'd be with her until something was definitely settled. That seemed the mother's self-appointed role.

When she came level with the barn she looked deliberately towards it, and there standing outside was Mike, and his gaze was brought sharply from the distance by the sight of her. She would have kept walking on but his voice, sharp and commanding, said, 'Mary Ann! Wait ... wait.'

When he came up to her he looked down into her face before speaking, and then he said quietly, 'Again it's not what you think, they just happened to be passing and saw me.'

83

She returned his penetrating look as she answered derisively, 'Da, don't be so silly.' She watched the colour deepen in his face, and now he growled, 'I'll have you remember who you're talkin' to; you seem to have forgotten lately.'

His angry tone did not upset her as it once would have done, and she replied defiantly, 'Well, who's fault is that? You said they were just passing. We're miles off the beaten track. Why would they be coming this way if it was not to see you? Don't tell me they were taking a walk right from Pelaw.'

'I don't know what they were doing, but they told me just that, that they were out for a walk. . . . You don't believe me?' His voice was quiet now and she hesitated a moment before replying. 'No, Da, I can't. . . .' Then, her voice almost gabbling, she rushed on, 'How can I believe anything you say when you're out two nights a week or more and you never used to go, and me ma nearly demented, and you not opening your mouth to her, except to talk at her. . . . Don't you see what you're doing to her? Don't you?'

'I'm doing nothing to her; it's her imagination that's doing it to her . . . and yours.'

'And mine? Then why did you say on the night of the wedding that you'd finish it if there was nothing to it? Why?'

'You can't finish what hasn't started, can you?'

'But you admitted it then . . . you did.'

Mike dropped his head and raised his hand to it, and, moving his finger across his wide brow, said tensely, 'Mary Ann, don't make me lose me temper. I've told you, I've told you more than once, there's nothing in it; but I'll be damned if I'm going to insult two nice people just to please you an' your mother and make meself out a bloody fool into the bargain. And what makes me more determined on this point is that neither of them has ever said a wrong word against you, or Lizzie. Just the reverse; they've had nothing but praise for the whole family. . . .'

'Oh, be quiet, Da, be quiet.' Mary Ann was now cupping her ears with her hands, pushing her hat awry as she did so. 'You're talking like a young lad. Even Corny would laugh at that. And me . . . I'm not very old but I know that's one of the oldest of women's tricks in the world. They're clever, both of them ... clever, and you're a fool, Da, a fool.' She stepped back from the angry glare in his eyes and the pressure of his voice as he cried, 'Mary Ann!'

'I don't care, I don't care, somebody's got to tell you. Do you know what they are?' She pressed her lips tightly together before she gave vent to the word, 'Bitches! That's what they are, a pair of bitches.' She didn't wait for his reply to this, but, turning from him, ran up the road. And it wasn't until she neared the main road that she drew to a walk. Her body was smouldering with her temper, and when, leaving the lane, she saw Yvonne and Mrs. Radley waiting for the bus, it needed only this to ignite it into flame.

What would have been the outcome of the meeting had the bus not arrived at that moment is left to surmise, but the look that Mary Ann bestowed on both of them as they turned smiling faces towards her must have warned them that their tactics and polite conversation were going to be lost on this particular member of the Shaughnessy family. They mounted the bus before her and took their seats together on the right-hand side. There was a double empty seat in front of them, but she ignored this and sat next to a woman on the opposite side. The woman alighted at the next stop and Mary Ann moved up to the window and sat looking out, telling herself that if they didn't get off before her she would pass them without as much as a glance.

But they did leave the bus before her; they alighted on the outskirts of Pelaw, and for a moment she saw them standing on the pavement, from where they looked straight at her and she back at them before snapping her gaze away as the bus moved forwards.

And apparently she wasn't the only one who had looked at them through the window, for almost immediately she became aware of the voice of one of the women sitting behind her, saying, 'Did you see who that was?'

'Yes,' answered the other. 'Ma Radley and her insurance policy.' At this the two women laughed, and Mary Ann said to herself, 'Insurance policy?' They were referring to Yvonne, but insurance policy ... she just couldn't get it. She strained her ears now to hear their conversation, but because of the noise of the bus only isolated words came to her, and these didn't make sense and could have referred to anything. But it was at the next stop that she heard something that brought her sitting upright in her seat. The woman who had first spoken said, 'Two she's had; the second's in a home, and they tell me the mother has an old bloke lined up now.'

'Two she's had.' Mary Ann repeated. That could have meant men, but the words 'The second's in a home' didn't apply to men, it applied to children, babies. She turned round quickly and looked at the women, and they brought their eyes from each other and looked back at her. She noticed that they were very nicely dressed, very respectable-looking. One of them flushed and glanced quickly at her companion; then, looking out of the window, she said, 'We're here,' and on this they both rose to their feet and left the bus.

And Mary Ann left it also. Almost as it was about to move off she jumped from the step.

'Excuse me.' She was breathless when she came to their side. 'Please' – she moved her head now – 'I know it's awful, but I was listening. I heard what you said about . . . about Mrs. Radley and her daughter. . . .'

'Now look here.' The taller woman pulled in her chin – an indignant motion. 'We were merely discussing something private.'

'I know, I know, but this is important to me. I wonder if you could tell me anything. . . .'

'No! It's none of our business what other people do.' The indignation was righteous now. 'And you shouldn't listen to people's conversation.'

'Then you shouldn't talk about them, should you?' Mary Ann thrust her chin up at the woman. Then, reminding herself that this attitude would get her nowhere, she said in a softer one, 'I just wanted to know if—'

'You'll get no information out of me. If you want to know anything about Mrs. Radley or her daughter why don't you go and ask them?'

On this the taller woman turned away and, after a quick glance at Mary Ann, her companion joined her.

Mary Ann stood on the pavement. She stood biting her

86

thumbnail and watching the women walking away. She watched them cross the road, pass three streets and then pause before the taller woman went up a side street while the other woman continued along the main road.

Intuition was Mary Ann's second nature, and now once again she was running. And when she came abreast of the woman she crossed over the road in front of her and waited for her approach.

'I'm sorry,' she began immediately, 'but ... but will you help me? It's important. You see ...' She paused, and, looking at the straight face of the other woman, she realized that only stark truth would get her anywhere, so she went on rapidly, 'Well, the old man your friend referred to is ... is me father.'

The woman's face softened and she nipped at her lip before saying, 'Oh, lass, I'm sorry, but it's no business of mine. An' you were right, we shouldn't have said anything.'

'Oh, please, please, don't mind that. I'm so glad you did. But the Radleys ... well, you see they are causing trouble; me ma's in a state.'

The woman shook her head in sympathy. 'I bet she is, poor soul. Look' – her voice dropped to a whisper now – 'don't stand here. I just live round the corner; come on in for a minute.' But before she moved away the woman glanced surreptitiously over her shoulder as if she expected to see her friend appear again. Then, as if by way of explanation, she said, 'I ... I wouldn't like her to think I'm doing anything behind her back. You understand?'

'I understand,' said Mary Ann, nodding her head quickly.

Again the woman felt there was need for explanation, and as she walked quickly up the street she went on, 'She's my friend and she has a lot to say, but when it comes to the push she'll never stand by it. I know more about the Radleys than she does, but I don't let on, I just let her have her say. ... Well, here we are.' She fumbled in her bag for her key, and after opening the door she stood aside to allow Mary Ann to enter.

It was a nice house, Mary Ann decided at once, clean, spanking clean, and orderly.

'Sit down,' said the woman as she herself took off her hat and coat. 'Well now.' She took a seat opposite to Mary Ann and she poked her chin out as she said, 'You look so young, hinny, for your da to be such an old man.'

'But he's not old, not really, he's just turned forty.'

The woman now screwed up her eyes. Then, her lips pressing together, her face expressed a knowing smile. 'Forty?' she said, on a high note. 'Well, that puts a different side to it, for the man that goes to the Radleys, well, he'll never see sixty again, not by a long chalk, although, mind, he's pretty spruce. You see. . . . .' She wriggled her buttocks to the edge of the chair. 'How I know all this is because me daughter lives two doors from them. I get all me news from her, but I don't let on to me friend.' She nodded towards the door now as if to indicate her friend. 'I always say Peggy tells me nothing – that's me daughter – but this old boy has been going to the Radleys, as far as I understand, for the last three months or so. You see, Ma Radley wants to get her married off . . . Yvonne I mean. I always said the French name went to her head, because she was like a march hare when she left school. Our Peggy was at the same school but she was a bit older. And then she had the bairn afore she was sixteen . . . I don't mean our Peggy, I mean Yvonne, you understand?' She was smiling at Mary Ann, but Mary Ann did not return the smile, for her face was set in a blank, fixed stare, and her mouth opened twice before she repeated, 'A baby! She had a baby?'

'Oh, aye, two, and by different fellows. That's why Ma Radley won't let her out of her sight. I've got no room for her at all . . . I mean Ma Radley, but I must admit she's had a handful with that girl.' The woman, warming to the theme, was becoming colloquial, her speech thickening with the northern inflexion as she went on, 'Then the second one she had last year. The man was married and he was made to pay for the bairn. And that one's in a home, sort of, because Ma Radley wouldn't have it in the house. But her first one was to a lad no older than herself, in fact not as old, and they couldn't do much about that. Anyway, he's skedaddled. But that one was adopted. Oh, she's been the talk of the neighbourhood, has that madam. But now I think this second business has scared her a bit because she's letting her mother hold the reins, so to speak. There's no coffee bars for her now an' coming home at two in the morning. And, of course, now it's pretty hard on her because none of the lads around here or in the factory wants her ... except for one thing, and perhaps she's realized that twice is enough; anyway, everybody's just been waiting to see if she snaffles the old boy. Mrs. Radley gave it out that he was her uncle, but it's funny that nobody round the doors heard of the uncle up till a few months ago. As for the old boy, well, he must be barmy thinking he can hold a young girl like her. But then all men of that age are barmy, aren't they?' She waited for an answer, and when none was forthcoming she made an inquiring movement with her head and said, 'And your da, hinny, he's gone on her, is he?'

'No,' Mary Ann denied firmly what she knew to be true. 'No, but she keeps ... they keep coming to the house. My mother and father met them at a holiday camp, you see, and as far as I gather she made a set at me da. ...'

'Oh, aye, she would that, anything with trousers on. And you don't think he knows about the bairns?'

'Oh no.' Mary Ann shook her head. 'I'm sure of that.' And she was sure of that. Her da, she would swear, had no knowledge of this wonderful piece of news, and to her at the moment it was a wonderful piece of news. If he had known about her having a baby ... in fact two babies and getting rid of them as it were, that would have finished anything before it had begun, because he himself had been brought up ... not in a home, but in the workhouse, left at the gate when only a few weeks old, without even a name pinned on him, and had been christened after the porter who had found him, Mike Shaughnessy. ... Oh no, there would have been no affair if Mike had known about the babies. Although she did not raise her eyes towards the ceiling, her whole being was looking upwards in thanksgiving. This, she considered, was the answer to her daily prayers over the past months.

She smiled now, saying, 'It's been good of you telling me this. You don't know what it means to me, what it'll mean to me ma.'

'Oh yes I do.' The woman nodded knowingly. 'And you tell your ma, it'll stop her worrying. He won't be such a fool when he knows the truth.'

Mary Ann rose to her feet, and although she said, 'Yes, yes, I'll do that, and thanks again,' she was already in two minds about passing her information on to her mother; she would have to think about it, talk it over with Corny. Yes, that reminded her, she was late already, she must hurry.

As she followed the woman along the passage to the front door she said again, 'You don't know how thankful I am.' And the woman, on opening the door, said, 'I can give a good guess, lass. Anyway, I hope everything turns out all right for you.' She dropped her head to one side now. 'If you're passing this way any time I'd like to hear how things turn out. Will you call in? Oh, except on a Friday.' She laughed selfconsciously. 'My friend comes round on a Friday; we have tea and go to the pictures.'

'Yes, all right. Yes, I will. Thank you.' Mary Ann was now in the street, and she looked at the woman where she stood above her on the step and said again, 'Yes, I'll drop in and tell you. Good-bye.'

'Good-bye,' said the woman; then added quickly, 'Oh, by the way, what's your name?'

Mary Ann hesitated. She realized now she had hoped to get away without revealing her name. 'Shaughnessy,' she said.

'Oh,' said the woman; 'Shaughnessy. It's an unusual name. . . . Well, bye-bye and good luck.'

'Bye-bye,' said Mary Ann.

By the time she had waited for another bus she was half-an-hour late when she reached the garage and she fully expected Corny to explode before she had time to explain what had delayed her. But Corny, standing in the wide doorway of the barn-like structure, greeted her with a smile. He did not even say 'You're late'; what he did say was, 'It's done, clinched.' He was breathing fast.

'No!' said Mary Ann, forgetting her own news in this moment.

'Aye, it all happened like that.' He snapped his fingers. 'When I came along this morning he was still for holding out, saying the road might come through this way next year; he'd had a hint of it, he said.' And now Corny's voice fell to a whisper and he pulled her further into the garage as he went on: 'When I got here this afternoon, his daughter was on the scene and had been arguing with him like mad. It appears that they are moving to Doncaster and she told him that if he didn't give up the place, then he would just have to get somebody in to look after him because they'd be gone within a fortnight. She told him to sell when he'd the chance, because if he was coming with them the place would be left empty and go to rot – she's like a good many more, she doesn't even believe the road will come this way. But, anyway' – he let out a long breath – 'he's put his name to the paper at last, and it'll all be fixed good and proper on Monday.'

'Did he come down?' Mary Ann asked him eagerly.

At this Corny lowered his head and kicked his toe gently against an oil cask as he said, 'No, just the reverse, he pushed me up another couple of hundred.'

'Aw, Corny.'

His head came up quickly. 'Look, I'm telling you, even at that it's a clinch. Just you wait, give me a couple of years.'

'But that'll make it four thousand.'

'I know, but I can manage it . . . I mean I've got just about enough to put down. And look, Mary Ann, it's worth it.' He pulled her now from the shelter of the garage and on to the rough, gravelled front, where stood two petrol pumps, and beyond into the road, and pointing to the side of the main garage he said proudly, 'There, look at it, our house.'

It was as if he was showing her something she hadn't seen before; and she was looking at it now as if it wasn't a place she had seen before. There it stood, a red brick building, the lower part given over to what appeared like a shop window, with a space behind it big enough to hold a car, and about the same amount of space to the side which was blocked now by two garage doors looking badly in need of a coat of paint. Above this was the house, their future home. She knew it had four rooms, a bathroom and a lavatory, but she had never seen them. She slipped her hand through his arm and, squeezing it, said, 'When can we go up?'

91

Corny looked down at her and said softly, 'He'll be out by Wednesday – his daughter's insisted on that – so we can get the place done up, at least as much as we can do in a week. But it'll be enough to start with, eh?' His voice had dropped to a whisper and she nodded back at him and answered as quietly, 'Yes, yes, it'll be enough to start with.' Their arms pressed close together, he said, 'Come on, I want to go and tell me grannie, and then we'll go home and tell Mike and your ma, eh?'

It was as they rode into Jarrow on the bus that she told him about the episode with the woman, and the knowledge she had come by.

Corny was wide-eyed as he looked down at her, and there was almost a touch of awe in his voice as he said, 'You were right about her, what she meant to do, I mean. If she's done it twice she could do it again, and with a fellow like Mike and how he feels about bairns . . . well. But now this'll clinch it, he'll get her measure now. But how are you going to tell him?'

'I don't know,' Mary Ann said, and she didn't. 'But,' she went on, 'I don't think I'll tell me ma yet, for somehow I imagine she would feel worse about it than ever. She'd likely get frightened that he might be more sympathetic towards her simply because she's had the two babies. I don't think he would, but me ma doesn't think like me, I know that.'

'Why not tell me grannie?' said Corny. 'She might come up with some idea of how to use it, I mean the information. She's wise, is me grannie, about these things; she's had a lot of experience you know.'

'I know,' said Mary Ann. And yes, she thought, if anybody could tell me how to go about this it would be Mrs. McBride.

'Name of God!' said Fanny. 'That should put the kibosh on it. Two bairns you say? God Almighty! She's got a nerve has that one, whoever she is. But I should say it was more the mother to be feared than the girl, although she couldn't do any damage without the daughter. Well now.' She looked across the table to where sat Mary Ann and Corny, side by side, and she said, 'It takes some thinking about, this. You ask me what you should do. Well, as I see it at the moment it's this way, and I'm speaking now with my knowledge of

Mike. Now were you to put this to him gently, and give him time to think, begod, it might have the opposite effect altogether and put him in sympathy with her. You never know men . . . oh no, you never know men, even the best of them. And another thing: if she's given time she'll like explain the whole thing away with a wet eye; there's nothing like tears for turning a man's opinion, even against himself and his better judgement.' She moved her big head on her thick neck. 'No, as I see it, you've got to use surprise tactics . . . drop it like a thunderbolt when they're both there.'

Both there!' Mary Ann, her eyebrows raised, glanced at Corny. 'You mean tell her, or tell me da, in front of her?'

'Nothing short of it, as I see it. You've got to blow the lid off it with no lead up. An' you can do it in an easy, diplomatic sort of way.'

'I can?' Mary Ann again glanced at Corny before looking back at Mrs. McBride.

'Aye . . . aye, when they're here together you can just sort of inquire how the bairns are. You see?'

Mary Ann saw – oh, she saw – but she also saw she wasn't up to this task, and she said rapidly, 'Oh no, Mrs. McBride, not in front of them both, I couldn't. I could tell me da or . . . or I think I could go to her and tell her what I know, but . . . but to say it in front of them both . . . I . . . I couldn't.'

'Well now, please yourself. You've asked for my advice and I've given it to you. But do whatever you think is best.'

'She's right.' Corny was nodding down at Mary Ann. 'You go to Mike and tell him and give him time to think and he'll soften; in spite of him being brought up in a home – in fact that's what'll make him soften towards her, the very thing, and the Lord knows what the offshot will be. Then if you go to the girl she might call your bluff, and as me grannie says' – he nodded in Fanny's direction without looking at her – 'tears can have a knock-out effect especially if they're from a V.P. like she is. . . . V.P. has nothing to do with important persons, in this case it stands for voluptuous piece.' He grinned at her, but she wasn't to be drawn into smiling at his quip.

'But . . . but, Corny, I just couldn't.'

'There's another way,' said Fanny. 'You could tell your mother and perhaps she would do it. . . . Aw' – she screwed up her face dismissing the idea – 'but then it might look like spite comin' from Lizzie, and Mike being a man might hold it against her, you never know. They keep worms in their minds for years, men do.'

Mary Ann looked from one to the other now, her face wearing a sadness, and her voice matching her expression, she said, 'It's me wedding day a week come Saturday, and now I've got this to tackle.'

Corny made no comment, he just continued to look at her tenderly, but Fanny, pulling herself up from the table, stated flatly, 'That's life, Mary Ann, that's life.' And going to the hob, she picked up a huge brown teapot, from which she refilled their cups, but in silence now, and in silence they drank.

CHAPTER SEVEN

IT was again Sunday, and judging from Mary Ann's feelings it could have been the day of doom. She was still doubting very much whether the bombshell method, suggested by Mrs. McBride, was the right course to take. Yet the alternative ways in which she could use her information all seemed to have loopholes that could lead to further complications.

She should be highly delighted about Corny's deal and the fact that she would now have a home to go to when she was married, but this big event in her life was being overshadowed and pushed into the background by the weight of the knowledge she carried.

Her preoccupied manner had not been lost on her mother either, for Lizzie had said to her, 'Are you having second thoughts about the garage?' and although she had answered immediately, and emphatically, 'No, no, I'm over the moon,' she knew her mother hadn't believed her.

Then there was Corny's mother and father. They had said to her last night, 'How do you feel about it?' whereas, if her manner had been normal, there would have been no need to put this question. Not that she minded very much what Corny's parents thought, because she hadn't taken to either of them, Mr. Boyle least of all. And she knew she wasn't alone in her attitude, for Corny didn't like his father either, although he had never put his feeling into words. And with his mother he was impatient; and Mary Ann thought he had every right to be, for she never kept the house clean or her pantry well stocked, her excuse being that it was no use trying to keep a place clean where there were eight children, which also made it hopeless trying to keep any food in the house. Although Corny's mother was Mrs. McBride's own daughter, they had nothing in common, except perhaps their untidiness, because that, too, was Mrs. McBride's failing. But

95

of one thing Mary Ann was sure: Corny loved his grannie. He had always shown this by spending more time in her two rooms in Mulhattan's Hall than across the water in his own home in Howden, where, incidentally, he didn't often take her. But because he was excited about getting the garage they had gone over last night.

And then this morning, her mother, pushing her own trouble aside, had taken her into the front room and said gently to her, 'Don't worry, everybody is like this before their wedding, you're up and down. At times you don't know if you should go on with it.' She wouldn't have been surprised had her mother added, 'And it would be a good thing if some of us didn't.' But what she said was, 'This time next week it'll be over and' – she had smiled wryly – 'just beginning.'

Mary Ann had wanted to take her mother's hand in hers and say, 'But, Ma, it's not that I'm worrying about, it's you, and me da and . . . and what I've got to do this afternoon, because I still don't know if it's the right way to tackle this thing.' But she hadn't spoken and Lizzie had said, 'Go up and see Tony and Lettice.' And then she had added, 'It's a pity you went to first mass; if you had gone to eleven o'clock that would have filled the morning and made the time pass until he came. You always need to be reassured by the sight of them at this time.'

Mary Ann had stared at her mother in silence; she couldn't tell her that she was barking up the wrong tree.

But now the waiting was nearly over. It was close on three o'clock, and if they had caught the two-fifteen bus they should be here at any time. She looked around the room. All the family were present, and as her glance passed from one to the other she thought, It's getting like a play every Sunday afternoon, the stage all set waiting for the first act to begin . . . or perhaps, today, the last act.

It was raining heavily outside and blowing a bit of a gale, and the big fire in the open grate was doubly welcome. If she hadn't known how he was feeling it might have appeared that her da was enjoying the blaze, at least from the way he was sitting with his legs stretched out towards the tiled hearth, his pipe in his mouth, and his head in the corner of the winged chair. She could not see his expression, but she had no need to look at his face to know that it would be tight ... he was waiting.

Her mother was sitting back from the fire, more towards the window. She was knitting. She did not usually knit on a Sunday afternoon, she generally read. Not once did she turn her eyes towards the window, but Mary Ann knew that she, too, was waiting.

Then there was Michael and Sarah, seated as usual on the couch, their hands joined as naturally as if they were children. Looking at them, Mary Ann thought, Our Michael's changed, in this short time he's changed. He's all bubbly inside, yet relaxed. His main job, she felt, was to keep his happiness under cover, to stop himself from being too hearty. As for Sarah, her happiness formed a radiance round her. Mary Ann could almost see the light, and at the present moment it aroused just the slightest bit of envy in her. Sarah could be happy, she had nothing on her mind, nothing to worry her. ... Aw, Mary Ann Shaughnessy! Mary Ann now reprimanded herself sternly. Sarah nothing on her mind? With that handicap? Aw, well – she mentally shook her head at herself – what I meant was, her da's not in trouble, and she hasn't facing her what I have in the next hour or so.

At this moment Sarah, looking across at her, caught her eye. Michael's gaze also joined his wife's, and Mary Ann, gazing back at them, realized that they, too, were waiting, and that below their evident happiness there was anxiety.

And then there was Corny. Corny was holding the floor again. Like a master of ceremonies, he was to the forefront of the stage, and as if he knew there was a bad play to be put over he was doing his best to entertain the audience beforehand.

'Anybody can write pop songs: Lyrics they call them. God-fathers! They've got a nerve. It's a racket, 'cos they can pinch the tune from the classics. But they daren't go pinching some bloke's verse, they've got to pay for that. So what do they do, the smart lads? Well, they hash up these so-called lyrics.' Corny now threw himself into a pose and sang in an exaggerated but tuneful tenor voice, 'I ain't loved nobody since I loved you, and, 'coo Liza, you ain't half got me in a stew.'

Even Lizzie laughed, at least she laughed with her mouth; Michael and Sarah rocked together; and Mike, turning his head, cast a quizzical glance up at the big clown. As for Mary Ann, she held her hands tightly across her mouth, and as she laughed she thought. Oh, Corny, you're sweet. It wasn't the right adjective to describe her future husband, but it described his intention, the intention of his clowning.

Corny was demanding of the entire room now, 'I'm right, though . . . it is all tripe, isn't it?'

'Oh, I wouldn't say all.' Michael came back at him. 'There are some good lyrics.'

'Tell me them then. Go on, just one.'

'Oh, I can't think of any off-hand.'

' "Trees", for instance,' said Sarah.

' "Trees"!' Corny's voice was high. 'But that's as old as the hills; it was written over thirty years ago, it's got whiskers.'

Corny's eyes were now brought round to Mike's face where Mike was once again slanting his eyes towards him, and he pushed his hand in the direction of his future father-in-law, laughing heartily as he cried, 'You know what I mean, Mike. Anyway, you haven't got whiskers.' He turned once again to Michael. 'I'm meaning the modern stuff. Granted there are plenty of decent writers, but they don't get the chance. I tell you, it's a racket. As for writing lyrics, I've made up umpteen tunes on me cornet but do you think they'd ever be taken?'

'Have you written them down?' asked Michael.

'No, I haven't.'

'Then how do you expect them to be taken? Put them down and send them up, and then if they're rejected you'll be speaking from experience; as it is you're just speaking from hearsay.'

Corny turned his gaze upwards now as he scratched the back of his head, and his mood changing with mercurial swiftness, he said seriously, 'Aye, perhaps you're right. If I could put them down . . . if. But' – he now looked at Michael

– 'I can't read music.' He was grinning in a derogatory way at himself. 'I can make tunes up – I've got umpteen in me head – and can bring them through the wind, but that's as far as it gets. But anyway' – he moved his body impatiently – 'we weren't talking about tunes, we were talking about the words. Now Mary Ann there: do you think they would put any of her stuff to music?'

Michael now cast a glance in his sister's direction, and with brotherly appreciation he said, 'There's a chance, that's if she ever did anything good enough.'

'Oh!' Mary Ann's voice sounded indignant. 'Don't praise me, Michael.'

'Don't worry,' said Michael, 'I won't.' But he laughed gently at her as he spoke.

And then Corny came back at him, crying, 'She's done some good stuff. If she had any sense she'd keep sending it off, but she doesn't.' He bounced his head at her, and for a second they exchanged glances, and then he went on, 'Some of her prose is like poetry.'

'You don't say,' said Michael, with mock awe now.

'Aye, I do. It's always the same in families, it takes an outsider to see what's going on.'

'Well, that's soon going to be rectified,' said Michael. 'And then you'll be blind to all our good points, especially your wife's. . . .'

As the door-bell rang and cut off Michael's voice they all looked startled. It would seem that Corny had succeeded in his efforts during the last few minutes and had made them forget what they were waiting for, but now he stopped his fooling; his part for the present was finished, but he said 'Will I go?' And Lizzie nodded to him without raising her head. Sarah pulled herself further up into a straighter position on the couch, as did Michael, while Mike, leaning forward, knocked the doddle from the bowl of his pipe. Only Mary Ann made no move. She sat farthest from the door and to the side of her mother, and as the sound of footsteps came across the hall her heart began to race. She hardly saw the mother and daughter enter the room, for there was a mist before her eyes, and she was afraid for the moment she was going to faint, or do something equally silly. That was until she saw Corny's face. His expression soft, his eyes were looking at her over the heads of the others, saying, 'It's all right, it'll soon be over.'

'What a day!' said Mrs. Radley. 'And how are you, Lizzie?'

Lizzie had not risen to greet the guests, but she raised her eyes and, looking at Mrs. Radley, answered, 'Quite well, thank you. ... I wonder that you ventured out in such weather.'

'Oh' – Mrs. Radley swung her permed, bluey-grey head from side to side, dismissing the weather – 'we like to get out. We must get out.' She leaned towards Lizzie now. 'We're not like you all here, we're not so fortunate as to have open land all round us; and when one loves the country, it's a great strain on the nerves being hemmed in by brick walls.'

Yvonne Radley was standing to the side of her mother; she had not addressed anyone in the room as yet. Her eyes had gone straight to Mike as soon as she came through the door. He'd had his back towards her, but now, when he turned to her, there was a defeated look about him; yet at the same time his eyes spoke of the anger he was feeling, anger at the combined attitude of his family and the obvious hostility filling the room. Getting to his feet, he said, 'Sit down.'

'Thanks ... Mike.'

Yvonne's hesitation in saying Mike's name suggested to Mary Ann's disturbed mind an endearing familiarity. She watched her father pointing to the couch and saying to Mrs. Radley, 'Sit down, won't you?' And as he spoke his angry glance was directed towards his son, for Michael, although he had risen reluctantly to his feet on their entry, had not offered his seat to the visitors.

'We are not going to stay long. We merely come with an invitation.'

Mary Ann's gaze, which had been directed towards her hands, snapped upwards now to Yvonne Radley, but the girl, a simpering expression on her face, was still looking at Mike and holding his attention as she went on, 'You see, it's my birthday on Wednesday and we'd like you to come along in the evening. We're having a little party.' She paused; then, her eyes flitting to Lizzie, she added with a girlish laugh, 'All of you I mean, of course, that's understood. . . . Will you?'

Lizzie now laid down her knitting and looked across the room at this girl for a full minute before answering her. She took in once again her long legs, her high bust, her round blue eyes, her simpering expression, her hair hanging like burnished bronze on to her shoulders, and as she looked she had the fearsome urge to spring on her, grip her by the throat and bang her head against the wall. The thought was terrifying in itself and it affected her voice as she answered, 'I'm . . . I'm sorry, but I have an engagement for next Wednesday evening.'

The word engagement seemed so out of place, the excuse so evidently an excuse that it actually created a wave of embarrassment among all those present, with the exception perhaps of the Radley's themselves.

'How old will you be?' It was Corny speaking now. His voice rough-edged, his face straight, he looked directly at the girl, and she, returning his look with a searching one of her own, answered, 'Nineteen.'

'Oh, Mary Ann's got a couple of months up on you.'

'Yes . . . yes.' Yvonne smiled now across the room at Mary Ann, and Mrs. Radley, following her own reasoning, put in quickly, 'Yvonne's got an aunt who is only sixteen. That's funny, isn't it? Yvonne nineteen, with an aunt sixteen.' She beamed from one to the other.

'Would you like a cup of tea?' Although Mike's voice sounded ordinary, his whole body looked stiff and defiant as he asked the question.

'Oh, no, Mike, don't bother; we won't stay,' said Mrs. Radley. 'We set out to have a nice long walk and we'll carry on. The weather doesn't deter us. . . . does it, Yvonne?'

'What?' Yvonne brought her gaze from Mike's averted face, then said, 'No, no. No, we love tramping. I love open spaces.'

As Corny, the devil in him, began to whistle softly, 'Oh give me a home where the buffalo roam,' Mike turned a fiery glance on him, and Corny allowed the tune to fade slowly away, but not too slowly, then went and stood beside Mary Ann and imperceivably nudged her with his arm.

Mary Ann did not need any nudging to be reminded of what she had to do. But how? How was she to start? She became panicky when she saw Mrs. Radley rise to her feet, followed by Yvonne. She had never expected them to go so soon, they had only just arrived. She couldn't do it – not in a hurry like this, anyway. She glanced at Lizzie sitting frozen-faced beside her, and it was the sight of her mother's patent unhappiness that loosened her tongue.

'Are you having many to the party?' Her voice was high and unnatural sounding, and she was conscious of everyone turning their eyes towards her, for never had she addressed either of the Radley's since their first visit.

'Well, no.' Again the simpering attitude from Yvonne. 'Only friends, close friends.'

Mary Ann gathered saliva into her dry mouth and swallowed deeply before she said, 'But you'll be having the children . . . the babies?'

There, it was done. The fuse was lit.

From the time the match is put to a fuse until the actual explosion takes place there is a period of comparative silence. This silence now filled the room; and as all eyes were once more turned towards her she had the desire to scream and break it. She saw the mother and daughter exchange a startled glance; then they were looking at her again, their eyes seeming to be spurting red lights towards her. The knowledge of exposure had been in their flicking glance, and it brought trembling power to her, and she said now, addressing Yvonne pointedly, 'Oh, of course, you mightn't be able to bring your eldest, him being adopted, but the baby you could; they'll let you have him from the home for the day, won't they?'

'Yo-u! . . . yo-u!' Yvonne took two rapid steps forward, but was checked from advancing farther by her mother crying, 'Stop it, Yvonne!' Mrs. Radley had gripped her daughter's arm and now, turning her white-strained face towards Mary Ann, she said, 'I don't know what you mean?'

'I think you do,' said Mary Ann, her voice more normal

sounding now; 'and so does she. Or would you like me to explain further?'

Yvonne Radley, pulling herself from her mother's grasp, gripped the head of the couch and, leaning forward over Sarah towards Mary Ann, hissed, 'You swine! You prying, sneaky little swine.' And now her tone was no longer recognizable, nor yet her expression. 'You think you're smart, don't you? You pampered, undersized little brat you. For two pins I'd....'

'You'd what?' said Corny.

'Yvonne! Yvonne! Stop it.' Mrs. Radley was now pulling at her daughter's arm, and the girl, angered with frustration and disappointment, burst into tears. Her wide, heavily painted mouth agape, she spluttered, 'I'll ... I'll get me own back on you, you'll see, you little upstart you. I hated you from the minute I clapped eyes on you ... you ...'

'Come away, come on.' Mrs. Radley's voice, piercing now, seemed to verge on hysteria, as she cried to Mary Ann, 'You haven't heard the last of this, miss, oh no. Oh no, not by a long chalk. You'll hear more of this; up for defamation of character, you'll see. You'll see, you nasty minded little —.' Mrs. Radley used a term which no one, judging from her previous refined manner, would have dreamt she ever knew – 'That's what you are, nothing else, a nasty minded little —. Come on. Come on. You'll not stay here another minute.' She pulled her daughter through the doorway into the hall, and nobody in the room made a move to follow them and let them out of the house.

The feeling of apprehension and worry which had filled Mary Ann since hearing Mrs. McBride's suggested method on how best to deal with the information concerning the Radley's was nothing compared with the terror filling her as she looked at her da. She was unaware of the others looking at her, their expressions all different. There was admiration in Michael's and Sarah's eyes; there was love and concern in Corny's; there was a look of amazement, mixed with pity and incredulity on her mother's face; but she saw none of these, she only saw Mike's face filled with black anger; it seemed to ooze from him. She fancied she could smell it, and her mind gabbled: He must have been in love with her. It was serious then. Oh dear Lord. As she watched him coming slowly and heavily towards her, she trembled with this new fear, fear of her da and what he was going to do to her. Now he was towering over her, his body stretched, his muscles hard and his one fist clenched. His jaw moved a number of times before his mouth opened to speak; then he said in a terrible tone, terrible because it was quiet, 'You think you've done something clever, don't you, Little Miss Fix-it? You've torn out somebody's innards and held them up for inspection. She had sinned, hadn't she? not once, but twice, so you, the good Catholic little miss, must—'

'Mike!' It was Lizzie's voice, commanding, loud, and it brought Mike's head swinging towards her, and, his voice no longer quiet now, he barked, 'You! . . . You! I'm warning you. You be quiet. It's you who started this, you and your fancies. And you see what you've brought her to, because she did it for you. She's turned into a sneaking little righteous ferret. So do what you've been doing for many a week, keep your mouth shut.'

And Lizzie kept her mouth shut, tight now, in a proud, bitter line.

Mike was again looking at Mary Ann, and, his tone dropping once more, he addressed her, saying, 'You're not out of the wood yet, me girl; marriage won't make you immune from emotions. Well, now' – he pushed his shoulders back even further – 'you intended to fix it for her, didn't you? Well, perhaps you have. Perhaps you've done just that . . . the lot of you, among you.' He flicked his eyes around the room before again levelling them on Mary Ann and going on: 'There's an emotion you know very little about as yet, me girl. It's called compassion, an' it can do very odd things, especially with an . . . old . . . man' – he stressed the old – 'an' a young lass saddled with two bairns.' He paused now, and into the pause Mary Ann whimpered, 'You wouldn't, Da, you wouldn't. Oh, I'm sorry, for what I did, but you wouldn't, you wouldn't.'

'Wouldn't I? Well, just you wait and see, me girl. I'm going to finish what you and your mother started. It's always good policy to finish a job, isn't it?'

Mary Ann, still staring at Mike, heard her mother's sharp

intake of breath, and it was as if she had leapt inside Lizzie's body and was retaliating for her, because now, of a sudden, she cried up at Mike, 'Well then, go on, go on, what's stopping you? Everybody wants to laugh out loud; they've been smothering it for weeks, so go on, and they can let it rip. You with your neck all creasy' – she pointed up at him – 'and big brown freckles on the back of your hand, which are not freckles at all, but the first signs of age coming on they say; and there's grey in your hair, but you can't see it at the back of your head, the same as you won't be able to see yourself as a doddery old man when you're left home here with the bairns while she goes . . .'

As the hand came across her face she thought that her head had left her body. She was conscious of herself screaming as she toppled backwards over something hard, then there was noise and yelling all about her.

As she felt her mother's hands raise her head from the floor the mist cleared from her eyes and she saw, standing like two giants within the open doorway, Corny and her da. They stood close together. Corny had hold of Mike's lapels, and Mike, his good arm sticking out at an angle from his body, was saying in that terrible voice again, 'Take your hands off me, boy.'

'YOU . . . You shouldn't have done that.' Corny's voice, too, was deep and unnaturally quiet, but his anger was causing him to stammer. 'If . . . if you were . . . weren't . . .'

'I told you . . . take your hands off me.'

'Corny! Corny!' Michael was now tugging at Corny's arms. 'Leave go. . . . Do you hear?' With a quick, strong pull he wrenched one of Corny's hands from Mike's coat and slowly Corny relinquished the other.

Mike now, taking a step backwards, lifted his hand and straightened his collar and tie while straining his neck upwards, and as he did so he looked at the two young men confronting him, both faces, that of his son and his future son-in-law, full of dark hostility. With a movement that seemed to lift his body completely from the floor he swung round, and the next sound that came to them was the banging of the front door.

Corny shook his head as if coming out of a dream; then,

turning swiftly, he went across the room to where Mary Ann was being supported by Lizzie, with Sarah in an unwieldy position on the floor at her other side.

'Don't cr . . . cry. Don't cry.' He was still stammering.

'Lift her on to the couch,' said Lizzie in a toneless voice. 'She's hurt her hip on the side of the chair.'

Corny lifted Mary Ann from the floor as if she were a child, and, seating her on the couch and still with his arms about her, he pressed her head into his shoulder, and it was the warm comfort, the understanding pressure of his arms, that released, in full flood, the agony in her mind – the agony of the knowledge that her da had hit her. Her da! . . . Corny, Mr. Lord, Mrs. McBride, or even Father Owen could have struck out at her – fantastic as the assumption was, she could have stretched her imagination to see it happening – but never, never her da.

'Don't, don't cry like that. Mary Ann, do you hear me?' Lizzie's hands had turned her face from Corny's shoulder and were cupping it. 'Stop it now.'

'Oh, Ma! M . . . ma!' She was spluttering and jabbering incoherently as she had done at times when a child and her world had broken apart. But now she was no longer a child, and things, some things, were more difficult to say; the words were sticking in her gullet, 'He . . . he . . . Ma.'

'Give over, child, give over.' It was as if Lizzie, too, was seeing her as a child again; and now she said to Corny, 'Carry her up to bed, will you?'

As Corny picked her up in his arms she turned her head towards Lizzie, crying, 'Ma, he . . . he didn't mean it.'

'There now, don't fret yourself any more, go on.' Lizzie pressed Corny forward.

'He didn't, Ma, he didn't, I te . . . tell you. . . . Where's he gone? Our Michael . . . our Michael, go and find him. Go on, Michael.'

'All right,' said Michael. 'Don't worry, I'll go and find him.'

From somewhere behind Mary Ann now her mother's voice, no longer toneless, said quickly, quietly and bitterly, 'You'll do no such thing, Michael. Stay where you are. He's gone. Let him go and I hope I never see him again.'

As Corny lowered Mary Ann on to the bed she held on to him, crying hysterically now, 'See . . . see, I shouldn't have done it. She said it would be all right; your grannie, she said it'd be all right, and now, look. A bombshell, she said. Fancy Mrs. McBride saying that. . . . A bombshell, a bombshell. . . .'

CHAPTER EIGHT

LIZZIE didn't know how much past midnight it was; she couldn't recall whether it was Saturday, Sunday or Monday; she was only aware that she had reached the crisis of her life, and she was living in that crisis. Years ago she had almost walked out on Mike and gone to her mother's, but now he hadn't almost walked out on her . . . he had walked out, he had gone completely. Why had this happened? Was she to blame? If she had laughed at the whole thing, would it ever have reached this point of torment? But she wasn't made to laugh when the vital issues of life were being undermined. She was not one of those who could follow the advice given by the wise sages in the women's magazines; these wisdom-filled females who had never touched on the experiences on which, each week, they poured out their advice; and such advice: 'Your best plan is to ignore the whole situation'; 'Welcome her to the house, treat her as if she were your daughter.' Were there women anywhere who could follow such advice?

Well, it was over, he had gone. She looked at the clock. No one had wound it up and it had stopped at twenty-five past twelve. If he had been coming back he would have been here long before now. Yes, it was over. Then she should go up to bed, shouldn't she?

She couldn't face that bed. She didn't think she would ever lie in it again; happy or otherwise, they had shared that bed for close on twenty-five years. No, tonight of all nights she couldn't face that bed. She would stay where she was, by the fire. She leant her head back in the corner of the high chair and looked across to where Mike's chair, startlingly bare, faced her. 'Oh, Mike, Mike.' It was a wail, coming as it were from far back in the beginning of time, spiralling up through her being, choking her, strangling her with the agony of things past, good things past.

'Are you all right?' Michael's hand on her shoulder brought her upright in the chair, her own hands gripping her throat.

'I'm sorry; did I wake you?'

'No, no, I wasn't asleep.'

He was on his hunkers before her now, his eyes soft on her face. 'Go on up to bed, Mother, go on.'

'I couldn't, Michael. I'm all right here. Don't worry. You go on in to Sarah.'

'She can't sleep either.'

'It's the couch, it isn't long enough.'

'No, it isn't that.'

'Where's Corny?'

'Outside somewhere.'

Lizzie's eyes stretched slightly. 'Outside in this?' She listened for a moment to the howling of the wind and the steel-rapping of the rain on the windows. 'What's he doing out there?'

'I don't know, he just feels like that. He's upstairs one minute and outside the next. He's been like that for hours.'

'What time is it?' she asked.

'It's after one, nearly half-past I should say. . . . How is she?'

'She was still asleep a short while ago.'

'That tablet has done the trick. It'll likely put her out until the morning. . . . Michael.' Although Lizzie spoke her son's name she turned her face from him, and it was some seconds before she went on, 'Will . . . will you carry on the farm?'

And it was some seconds before Michael answered, 'Aw, Mother, you know I will . . . but . . . but it won't come to that. . . .'

'It'll come to it all right, Michael, let's face it. This is the end.'

'He'll come to his senses. You've got to give him a chance. He was mad at the way it happened.'

'I don't want him, Michael, when he comes to his senses. Once he has spent a night with that girl nothing on God's earth could make me take him back. I can't help it, that's how I'm made. I've never wanted anybody but him in my life, and up to now it's been the same with him. But . . . but it wouldn't be any use him crawling back when his madness has cooled off. No use at all.'

Her voice was so level and conveyed such finality that Michael knew that no persuasion would make any impression on his mother's attitude. As he pulled himself up straight a noise in the yard brought him sharply round, his face to the kitchen door. And Lizzie's head came up, too, at the sound of running steps. The next minute they heard the back door open, and within seconds Corny appeared in the doorway. The water was running from his plastered hair down on to his black plastic mack. He stood gasping for a moment wiping the rain from his face with his hand before coming farther into the room; then looking from Michael to Lizzie he brought out, 'He's back.'

'Me father?' It was a soft question from Michael, but Lizzie made no movement.

'Where?' said Michael now.

'I saw him going up into the loft. All night I had a feeling he was somewhere round the place. I looked everywhere, but no sign of him, yet I couldn't get rid of it, the feeling. And then it was Simon who gave me the tip. You know that little bark he gives when he sees him, or smells him. Well, I heard him come out from the lower barn growling and then there was this little bark, and I stood in the shelter of the byres and I saw the outline of him. He . . . he was swaying a bit. It could be that he's got a load on, yet I don't know. But I didn't go near him.' He jerked his head to the side. 'After what happened he wouldn't welcome the sight of me.'

'I'll get the lantern.' Michael was running across the room; then at the door he turned and said to Corny, who was about to follow him, 'Don't come. Stay with me mother.' And he cast a glance in Lizzie's direction before hurrying out of the room.

Getting to her feet, Lizzie went and stood before the fire, with her hand lifted to the mantelpiece and her head bowed. It was a stance she often took up when deeply troubled.

After some minutes of silence Corny approached the fire, but not too near to her; and holding his hand out to the warmth, he said softly, 'I feel that I'm to blame as much as anybody for what has happened, Mam. You see, when Mary

Ann told me and said she didn't know what to do, I mean about letting on about what she knew, I told her that the best one to go to for advice was me grannie, and it was me grannie who suggested that she make her information into a bombshell. I can see now it was wrong, but . . . but you can always be wise after the event, can't you?' He waited a moment, and when no answer came to him he lowered his head and muttered, 'I'm sorry.'

Lizzie turned towards him now and, putting out her hand, touched his arm. 'Don't blame yourself, Corny,' she said. 'If you want to know something, I think it's just as well it happened like this. It had to come to a head sooner or later. It had to burst.'

'What'll happen now?' he asked softly. 'You'll not take it out of . . .?'

Turning from him, Lizzie said abruptly, 'We'll just have to wait and see, Corny, won't we? We'll just have to wait and see. . . .'

They were standing in silence, finding nothing more to say, when Michael came hurrying back into the kitchen. It seemed that he could not have been as far as the big barn in so short a time. He, too, was gasping with his running against the wind, but he came straight to Lizzie, where she stood on the hearthrug waiting, and straight to the point, saying, 'He's in a bad way, Mother, he's—' He shook his head slowly. 'He's never been out of the fields. He's covered with mud from head to foot and wet to the skin; the things are sticking to him. He must have been headlong in the dyke down by Fuller's Cut. He's shivering as if he had ague.' He put his wet hand on her. 'He's never been away, you understand, not farther than the fields.'

Michael watched as his words slowly brought the colour back into his mother's face. He seemed to watch the years drop away from her. Her voice had a slight tremble in it as she said to him, 'Give me my coat, will you?' Then when Michael had brought her coat from the hall and helped her into it, she asked, 'Is the lamp outside?' And when he nodded, she said, 'Don't come with me.' Then, looking from him to Corny, she added, 'Go to bed, Corny – the spare bed is ready.'

Corny said nothing, and Michael said no more, but they both watched her as she swiftly pulled the hood of her coat over her head and went out of the room.

Having picked up the lantern at the back door, Lizzie battled her way across the farmyard towards the barn. When she reached the great doors she stood for a moment to regain her breath; then, pushing open the small hatch door, she bent down and entered the barn. As she walked unsteadily towards the ladder that led to the loft, the light from the lantern, and her steps, caused a scurrying of small creatures. Then she was on the ladder, mounting it slowly, and when she reached the top Simon's wet nose greeted her before he turned and ran to the far end of the loft, where a bale of straw had been broken and on which lay a huge, huddled figure.

As the light of the lantern fell on Mike, Lizzie paused. Her body still stiff and erect, her face still wet, she looked down on her husband, and with the exception of the empty sleeve no part of him was recognizable to her, but she was made immediately aware that the mud-covered shape was shivering from head to foot. Bending slowly over him, she touched his shoulder, and after a moment he turned his face towards her, only to turn it as quickly away again. Evidently he had not expected to see her.

It was the unguarded look in his eyes that softened the ice round Lizzie's heart, for the look reminded her of the dog they had found in Weybridge's cottage three years ago. The Weybridges were a no-good family who had lived off the beaten track about two miles over the fields, and whose debts had caused them to do a moonlight flit one night, and they had left their dog chained up in an outhouse. He was there a fortnight before Michael had found him and brought him home, and the poor creature had crawled on his belly across the length of the kitchen and laid his head across her feet. He was an old dog, and partly blind. Apparently he had been used to a woman and had immediately given to her his allegiance, and in return she had looked after him lovingly until he had died last year.

'Come on, get up,' she said softly. But Mike did not move. 'Do you hear me?' she said. 'Get on your feet.'

For answer he buried his face in the straw and muttered something which she could not hear.

Placing the lantern at a safe distance, she bent over him again, and, gripping him by the shoulder and using all her strength, she jerked him from his prone position. And now, with his head hanging, he muttered through his chattering teeth, 'Leave me be for the night, will you?'

'I'll do no such thing; get on your feet.'

'I ... I can't. I'm finished for the time being. I'll ... I'll be all right in the mornin'. Go on in, go on in.' He went to lie down again but her hands prevented him. 'Get up,' she said. 'Come on, get up.' Her voice was soft, pleading now, and after a moment he turned on all fours and raised himself up on to his knees, and then up to his feet.

She was appalled at the sight of him. As Michael had said, he must have fallen headlong into the muddy ditch at Fuller's Cut.

She guided his shaking form to the ladder, then on to it, and held the light aloft until he had reached the floor of the barn. Then descending quickly, once again she guided him, and when they were in the yard she put her arm about him to steady him against the wind, and with the docility of a child he allowed himself to be helped by her until they reached the back door, and there, stopping and pulling himself slowly from her grasp, he muttered, 'Are they in?'

'No, no,' she whispered hurriedly, 'they're all in bed.'

In the scullery he stopped again, and, looking down at the condition of himself, he brought out, his words rattling like pebbles against his teeth, 'I'll ... I'll change here.'

For answer she pulled off her coat, saying briskly, 'You're going straight upstairs into a bath.'

She led the way now, quietly through the kitchen, into the hall and up the stairs; and he followed, stepping gingerly, his limbs shaking with every step he took. But when they entered the bathroom and she had turned on the bath and pulled some warm towels from the rail, he said, without looking at her, 'Leave me be now, I can manage.'

When he felt her hesitation he added, in a tone that was more like his natural one, 'I'll be down when I'm tidied, leave me be.'

When Lizzie returned to the kitchen her own legs were shaking so she felt she must sit down before she dropped. But as she neared a chair she stopped, saying to herself, 'No, no, keep going, keep going.' She knew it would be fatal at this moment to sit down and think. If she sat down she would break down, and she didn't want that. He would need something hot, piping hot, if there wasn't to be repercussions to this state he was in. How long had he been wet through to the skin? Eight ... nine hours? And in this wind that was enough to cut through you like a sword! Hot bread and milk, she said, that will act like a poultice and ... She looked towards the store cupboard, seeing at the back of it, hidden among the bottles of sauces, mayonnaise and pickles, a flask of whisky. It had stood there a long, long time, waiting for an emergency; and this was the emergency. She had put her foot down on Mike having whisky in the house, yet she had always kept that flask hidden there. It was strange, she thought, as her hand groped knowingly over the shelf and brought out the bottle of Johnnie Walker, strange that she herself should give him whisky. ...

It was half-an-hour later when Mike came downstairs. When she heard his soft, padded approach her body began to tremble and she went hurriedly into the scullery and brought the pan of bread and milk from the stove, and she was pouring it into a basin when he entered the room. She did not look towards him; nor did Mike look at her, but, pulling the cord of his dressing-gown tighter about him, he walked to the fire and stood, very much as she had done earlier, looking down into it, his one hand gripping the edge of the mantelpiece.

Lizzie now opened the flask of whisky and poured a generous measure into a beaker, and after adding brown sugar to it she went to the fire and, bending sideways so that no part of her touched Mike, this seemingly back-to-normal Mike, she lifted the boiling kettle from the hob and, returning to the table with it, filled the beaker. Then, the kettle in one hand, the beaker in the other, she went once again to the fireplace, placed the kettle on the hob and, with her eyes fixed on the beaker as she stirred the hot whisky and sugar, said softly, 'Drink this.'

Without moving his body Mike brought his head round and looked at her, then at the beaker. The smell that came from it was of whisky, the liquor that was forbidden in the house, forbidden because of his weakness. The hot stinging aroma swept up his nostrils and down into his body. It was too much, too much. He took his hand from the mantelpiece and pressed it over his face, digging his fingers into his scalp as if he would tear the whole façade of his features from their base, and his body crouched forward and writhed in agony as he brought out her name, 'Liz. Oh, Liz.'

As she swiftly laid her hand on his bent head she had the feeling she was touching him for the first time. She could not see her hand or his head now; the ice fast melting round her heart was flowing from her eyes, bathing her face, and refreshing her soul like spring floods on a parched land. She put her arms about him and he clung to her fiercely while a torrent was released from him, too – a torrent which checked his speech and choked him yet could not stop him repeating her name over and over. And he asked forgiveness and said what he had to say with his hand as it moved in tight pressure over her head, her shoulders and her back. How long they stood like this they didn't know, but presently Lizzie muttered chokingly. 'It'll . . . it'll be cold.' Blindly she put out her hand to the side and lifted the glass from the mantelpiece and put it to his lips; and over the brim of it they looked at each other. Once again they were survivors, once again they had swum ashore. And with this rescue Lizzie was sure of only one thing: never again would Mike sail so near the wind, and never would he sign on, so to speak, in a vessel similar to the one that he had just escaped from.

That voyage was over.

As the late dawn broke Mary Ann came out of her drugged sleep. She lay for a moment quite still, staring towards the dim lines of objects in the room. She felt awful, her head ached; and as she thought of her head aching, she realized that her face was aching too, as if she'd had toothache, and her leg felt stiff. As she put her one hand to her face and another to her hip the reason for her aches and pains crept slowly into her mind and she groaned as she turned round and half buried her face in the pillows. Closing her eyes, she went over the scene of last night. She remembered crying and shouting after her da had hit her. She remembered that she couldn't stop, and that she had kept blaming Mrs. McBride for it all. That was just before her mother gave her that tablet; it must have been a sleeping tablet.

She turned on to her back again and looked towards the window. Mrs. McBride wasn't to blame, she herself was to blame. When she had found out about Yvonne Radley she should have gone to her mother with the news, or, failing that, she could have got her da on the quiet and risked the consequences. She felt a wave of sickness creep over her as she thought that, whatever she had done, the result couldn't have been any worse.

But what had happened since last night? Her mother left all alone. In this moment she had no doubt but that her mother had been alone all night, for remembering the look in her da's face she knew it meant defiance and going his own road. She must get up and see her mother.

As she pulled herself into a sitting position she thought, Oh dear, I feel awful, awful, and she lay back again, her head against the bed-head, listening for a moment to the usual household sounds that the dawn brought: the muffled steps rising from the kitchen below, a door closing, Simon barking, the lowing of the cattle . . . the cattle. She lifted up her head from its resting position. . . . Who'd look after the cattle, the farm as a whole? Michael, of course . . . Yes, there was Michael. Her head dropped back yet again. She must get up and find out what was going on, but oh, she felt awful.

She was pushing the bedclothes off her when there came the sound of footsteps on the landing; they were quiet, heavy and slow. Recognition of these steps brought her face round to the door. She paused with the bedclothes in her hand, one leg hanging over the side of the bed, and when the gentle almost imperceptible tap came on the door she pulled her leg back into the bed and the clothes about her and waited.

When the door opened and she saw her da enter, and he in his night things with his dressing-gown on, a cup of tea in his hand and a look on his face that she hadn't seen there for many a day, she wondered for a moment if she had died in the night, or if she was still dreaming? Or, if she was awake, was she being affected still by the sleeping tablet? She kept her eyes on him as he walked slowly to the bed. She watched him put the cup of tea on the table, then lower himself down on to the bed side. As she stared into his face the years slipped from her; she was seven again, or nine, or eleven, or thirteen, and she knew that in all the world there was no one like her da. There had never been anyone anywhere on earth like him before and there would never be again; yet in all their past comings together she had never seen a look on his face like now. She would have said her da knew nothing about humility; her da could never be humble, but within this big-framed, virile individual who was sitting before her now was a humble man, a shamed man, who was half afraid of how his gesture might be received. She watched him bring his hand to her face, to the painful side, and when she felt his fingers touch her cheek she hunched her shoulders and cradled his hand while her arms went swiftly up around his neck.

'I'll never forgive meself.'

'Forget it, oh forget it, Da. It was nothing. I asked for it.'

'I'll never forget it to me dying day.'

She pressed him from her and she looked at him, but she couldn't see him. And she asked him a question. It didn't seem necessary but she had to ask it. She had to hear him answer it. She said, 'Is everything all right, Da?' Dimly she saw the movement of his head, and then he held her again before he answered, in a thick murmur, 'Aye, thanks be to God.'

Thanks be to God, he had said, and her da didn't believe in God – well, not the recognized God anyway. ... But thanks be to God. And she, too, from the bottom of her heart, from the core of her being to which he had given life, she, too, said, 'Thanks be to God.' But aloud she responded in her usual way. 'Oh, Da! Oh, Da!' she said.

CHAPTER NINE

'You had better go on up,' said Lizzie, 'Mr. Lord will be waiting for you.'

'I will in a minute, Ma,' Mary Ann answered as she dashed through the kitchen and into the hall, calling from there, 'I just want to see the weather report.'

Lizzie smiled at Sarah where she sat in a chair to the side of the fire busily stitching, and she whispered down to her as she passed her, 'The weather report. The weather report for the third time today.' They laughed softly, exchanging glances, and then Lizzie went on into the front room, there to hear the announcer, who was seemingly talking solely to Mary Ann from the screen, telling her she had no need to worry, for he and God had conspired on her behalf to still the elements, and all would be bright and serene on the morrow.

Mary Ann turned and smiled at Lizzie as she came to her side, and she leant against her mother's shoulder, and Lizzie put her arm around her and squeezed her gently for a moment. Then, pressing her hastily away, she went and closed the front-room door and came quietly back; and, looking down at her daughter for a moment before dropping her gaze to the side, she said hesitantly, 'I've ... I've never spoken about last Sunday, and there mightn't be any more time before tomorrow, I mean ... I mean when we can be alone, but I want you to know' – she raised her eyes slowly – 'I want you to know how I feel. ...'

'Oh, Ma, don't talk about it, it's over.'

'I've got to talk about it, just this once; I've got to put into words that I'm grateful.' With her raised hand she hushed Mary Ann's attempt to speak, and went on, 'Perhaps it's the last thing you need ever do, in that way, for your da. I know now what it must have cost you to go through with it, because if it had gone wrong, as it could well have done, you would have blamed yourself to the end of your days. But as usual, where he is concerned, you took the right tack.'

'It wasn't me, it was Mrs. Mc...'

'I know all about that, my dear. But Mrs. McBride didn't do it. And you know something! I've got a feeling that all this just had to happen. ...' She paused, and her expression softened still further before she went on, 'I can say this to you because tomorrow you're going to be married. You've got a lot to learn, and as the years go on it'll get harder, not easier, but somehow I think you already know that ... you've had enough experience.' She smiled a small smile that Mary Ann returned. 'But this business has opened your da out ... I mean towards me, because he's never been the one to talk and try and get to the bottom of things; he's been afraid to, inside. And I know now that I haven't helped him much in that way; I close up like a clam. It's my nature, I suppose, and I've always told myself that I couldn't help it, but now I know it would have been better for both of us if I'd tried. Anyway' – she jerked her head – 'to cut a long story short, we've talked the last few days as we've never done in our lives before. We've gone deep into things, and the deeper we've gone the closer we've become; and as I see it, we've got you to thank for it.'

'Oh, Ma, no. No. Don't, don't go on.'

Lizzie leant forward now and kissed her daughter and they held each other tightly for a moment. Then pushing Mary Ann towards the door, Lizzie said in a voice that was not quite steady, 'Go on now, go on up. You don't want him to get annoyed, do you?'

Mary Ann made no answer to this, but, going swiftly into the hall, she grabbed up her coat from the hall-stand and went out by the front way.

The light from the cow-sheds was illuminating the yard as she hurried towards the far gate. She heard her da chastise Primrose, saying, 'Behave now, behave yourself.' Primrose was a milk chocolate, dappled, wide-eyed Jersey cow, and, unlike her eight sisters, she had a temper. Their Michael used to say that she herself was like Primrose both inside and out. She saw Michael now, his silhouette outlined against the window. He could be mistaken at a distance for her da. She made her way more slowly now, up the hill towards the brightly lit house standing on the brow, and when she entered the kitchen Lettice, wearing a large apron over her smart dress, turned to greet her. Ben was sitting to the side of the Aga stove, a small table at his hand, on which stood articles of silver that he was busily cleaning. She had never seen Ben with his hands idle. He gave her his tight smile, and Lettice, coming round the table and taking off her apron, said softly, 'Oh, I'm glad you've come, he's getting fidgety. Tony's with him now. He's had poor Ben here run off his feet all afternoon.'

'But it was only about an hour ago I got the message . . . I was coming up, anyway.'

'Well, you know what he is.' They smiled at each other, and then Lettice, leading the way into the hall, asked softly, 'Excited?' She turned and looked at Mary Ann. And Mary Ann, looking squarely back at her, said, 'No. I don't feel anything at all. It's as if I've had an injection, like after getting a tooth out, you know, just like that.'

Lettice laughed softly. 'It's the usual reaction.'

'I suppose so.' Mary Ann gave a little hick of a laugh. 'The only thing I've been concerned about today is to-morrow's weather.'

'Well, that's a good sign.' They were laughing quietly together as they entered the drawing-room.

'Oh, hello there.' Tony rose to his feet. 'Well, how goes it?'

Before Mary Ann could answer him Mr. Lord turned his steely gaze on her and remarked caustically, 'Taken your time, haven't you, miss?'

'I've been busy.'

'What about a drink?' said Tony. 'A glass of sherry or something?'

'No, no thanks, Tony.' Mary Ann shook her head. 'I'm not long after having my tea.'

'Don't encourage her to drink.' Mr. Lord now glared at his grandson. 'Sherry, sherry, sherry . . . I don't believe in this constant imbibing, and don't encourage her to start; she'll acquire enough bad habits after tomorrow.' Mr. Lord was staring towards the blazing fire as he spoke, and Lettice, Mary Ann and Tony exchanged glances.

Looking at Mary Ann but speaking to Mr. Lord, Tony said teasingly, 'I grant you she's very young, but we aren't and we need a drink.' And on this diplomatic reply he took Lettice by the hand and they went from the room, Tony winking at Mary Ann knowingly.

And now Mary Ann sat down facing Mr. Lord. They looked at each other in silence for some minutes, and as she stared at her benefactor – and benefactor he had been – the odd numbness that had been filling her all day quietly dispersed and she was filled, in fact overcome, by a feeling that could be described by no other name but love. She loved this old man, really loved him. Her feelings stretched out her hands to him, and when he grasped them they still remained in silence looking at each other. When at last she spoke, she said something that was quite unrehearsed, something she had never dared to say before. She said, 'I've never had a granda ... I mean I've never known one, either me mother's or me da's, and so inside I've always thought of you as me granda.'

The sagging muscles twitched, the lips moved, the creasy lids dropped over the eyes, then gently he drew her up from her chair and towards him, and then for only the second time in their acquaintance she found herself sitting on his knee. And as she lay with her head buried in his shoulder he talked to her. His voice no longer harsh or cutting, he said, 'You have not only been to me as a granddaughter, Mary Ann, you have also been a source of life. The day you came on to my horizon I was merely existing. ... You remember that day?' She made a slight movement but did not speak. 'And with your coming you restored my faith in human beings. Moreover, you brought me a family, because, you know, I look upon your mother and father, and Michael and Sarah now – as my family. You brought me Tony, and through Tony you brought me Lettice, which, contrary to my first opinion, has turned out to be a good thing after all. ... You've brought me all this and now you are going. Tomorrow, I could say, I am going to lose you. But no ...

no' – the bony frame moved in the chair – 'I'm not going to say that, Mary Ann, because I'll never lose you, will I?'

Her voice was cracked and high as she said, 'No, no, never.'

'There now, there now. Don't cry.' He blew his own nose violently, then added, 'I don't want to be browbeaten by Mr. Cornelius Boyle for upsetting you.' This was intended to be funny, and Mary Ann smiled at him as she sat up and wiped her face. Mr. Cornelius Boyle! Would he never call him Corny? No, never. That would be too much to ask. He was saying now, 'That reminds me. Look, there on the desk.' He pointed. 'There are two envelopes, go and get them.'

She slid from his knee and brought the envelopes to him, and when she put them into his hand he looked at them, then, handing one to her, he said, 'That is for you. I haven't bought you a wedding present, get what you want with it.' The envelope was addressed simply: 'To Mary Ann.' Then he handed her the other envelope, on which was written 'Mr. Cornelius Boyle', saying, 'This is for Cornelius. I always believe that a man and woman should share everything, happiness, money, and troubles, so I have made you both alike. I would have given this to him himself if he had honoured me with a visit, but one must make allowances, for he is a very busy man at the moment . . . a very busy man.'

Again he was attempting to be amusing, and now Mary Ann, flinging her arms around his neck, hugged him almost boisterously, and as she hugged him she whispered softly, 'I love you, I love you.' And she did.

'Go on. Go on.' He pressed her up from him; his head was lowered, and once again he was blowing his nose; and now through his handkerchief he said, 'I'll see you tomorrow.' And then he added softly, as he lifted his misted eyes towards her, 'Look beautiful for me, Mary Ann. Look beautiful for me.'

She could say no more, she could only stare at him for a moment longer before hurrying from the room.

In the hall she stopped and wiped her face and blew her nose; and while she was busy doing this, out of the morning room came Lettice and Tony. Apparently they had been waiting for her, and without speaking they took up a position on either side of her and walked with her into the kitchen and to the back door.

And now Tony took her face in his hands, and, bending solemnly towards her, kissed her, saying, 'Be happy, Mary Ann. And you will be, you deserve it. God bless you.' And as he turned away from her, Lettice put her arms about her and muttered something like, 'Thank you, Mary Ann; I hope you'll be as happy as you've made it possible for me to be.'

She was running quite blindly down the hill, completely choked with happiness. Everybody was nice. Everybody was being kind to her. Everybody was lovely. Look what her ma had said, and Tony and Lettice. But look what Mr. Lord had said. Oh, she loved him. She did, she did. . . .

She went headlong into the gate and winced with pain, and as she rubbed her leg, which was still sore from contact with the chair on Sunday, she said to herself, 'Wipe your face; don't go in like that. If our Michael sees you looking like that you know what'll happen, he'll give you a lecture on the feebleness of sentiment. Even when he's wallowing in it he won't spare you. You know our Michael.'

As she entered the scullery she heard Corny's voice coming from the kitchen, saying, 'Lord, I'll never get through, and I've got to go to confession, I promised Father Owen I would.'

'You should have gone with me last night, I told you.'

He turned to her, his eyes merry, his face bright. 'Stop nagging,' he said. And now he looked at Mike, who was standing with his back to the fire. 'Coo! What it's going to be like after, man. You know, I've got cold feet.' And now his merry tone changed and he added flatly, 'And no kiddin'.' As he finished speaking he held out his hand towards Mary Ann – the action in itself had an endearment about it – then, looking at her more closely, he asked, 'What's up?'

'Nothing, nothing.' She put her hand in her pocket. 'I've been up to the house. Mr. Lord's given us our wedding present, one each.' She handed him the envelope, and Corny, looking down at it, read aloud, 'Mr. Cornelius Boyle', then asked quietly, 'What's on yours?' She turned the envelope towards him and he read, 'To Mary Ann.'

'Funny, isn't it?' He glanced at Mike, and Mike nodded,

123

saying, 'It's one of the things you'll have to get used to, Corny. We've all been through it.' And half in fun and whole in earnest, he said, 'She's been . . . ours' – he had almost said 'mine' – 'only after she's been his, and the situation will remain the same after tomorrow. You'll have to get used to taking second place, lad.'

'Oh, Da.' Mary Ann chided him with her look; then she slit open the envelope. Inside was a cheque, nothing else, and the sum on it brought her mouth agape. She looked from the cheque to Corny and back to the cheque, and she whispered, 'It's for a thousand pounds.' Then, casting her eyes first to Lizzie, and then to Mike. she repeated again, 'A thousand pounds. Ma, look . . . look, Da.' She held the cheque out stiffly to them, and they looked at it. Then Mike, raising his eyes to Corny, where he stood slightly apart, his face wearing a blank look, said, 'Open yours, Corny.'

Slowly Corny opened the envelope and he, too, drew a cheque from it and his amazement and mystification when he saw the same sum written on it elicited the exclamation of 'God Almighty!' before he added below his breath, 'Why, he's givin' me the same, the same as you.'

Mary Ann nodded at him.

'A thousand.' Corny, his eyebrows pushing towards his hairline, shook his head; then on a higher note: 'A thousand pounds!' His head moved wider. 'Mike! Man! A thousand pounds! Two thousand atween us! Struth, I can't take it in.' He brought his eyes down to Mary Ann. Then his tone changing, he asked, 'Is it something he's up to?'

'No. No.' Mary Ann's voice sounded like a bark. 'Stop being suspicious of him. It's his kindness; he done it out of kindness and understanding. He . . . he said that a' – she could not bring herself at the moment to say husband and wife so substituted a couple – 'couple should always start off equal, that's what he said, and you go putting the wrong construction on it as usual.' Her voice was rising and was only checked by Corny lifting his hand in a very good imitation of Mike, saying, 'Enough. Enough.' As they all laughed, Mary Ann bowed her head and tried to suppress a grin. Then swiftly she raised it, and looking at Corny again she said quietly, 'But it's wonderful, isn't it?'

'Wonderful? That isn't the word. I'm simply floored.' He looked at the cheque once again. 'I've never seen a cheque for a thousand pounds, but, what's more, I just can't get over him givin' it to me. Why, you should have heard him when I was up there last time, I almost crawled out of the room. I mean I would have if I'd let myself be intimidated by him, he went for me left, right and centre. And now—' he waved the cheque, 'and now this. ... It's way ... way beyond me.'

'You'll have to go up and thank him,' said Lizzie.

'Yes, yes,' Mary Ann nodded emphatically.

'Aye. Yes, of course,' said Corny. 'Yet' – his mouth twisted into a wry grin – 'I'll need some practice. I don't know how I'll go about it. Anyway, I can't go now, as I said I've got to go into church, so I'll do it when I come back.'

'He'll be in bed then,' said Mike.

'Well, I won't be able to do it until tomorrow after . . .' He paused and looked softly towards Mary Ann; then asked her, 'Will that be all right then?'

'Yes. He doesn't know I'm seeing you tonight, anyway. You needn't have received it until tomorrow. But look, before you go' – she held out her hand – 'come and see what the girls in the office bought us.'

Corny allowed himself to be led into the front room, which had taken on the appearance of a combined linen and china shop, and there she pointed out to him an addition to the presents; it was a fireside chair.

'Coo! That's nice.' He sat in it and stretched out his long legs. 'It was decent of them, wasn't it, and you not being there long.'

'Yes, it was. They got it at cost from the firm; it's a very good one.' She patted the back near his shoulder, and Corny, looking at her, his eyes almost on a level with hers, turned the subject by asking her quietly, 'How do you feel?'

'Aw, well. You know. ...' She gave a sheepish grin, shrugged one shoulder, then lowered her head a little. 'I don't believe it's happening to me. It's as if all this' – she waved her arm about the room – 'was for somebody else. One thing I can't take in is that it's . . . it's my last night here . . . in this house.'

'You're going to miss it.' He was staring straight-faced at her now. 'Our place is nothing like this. Even when we get it all fixed up it still won't be like this; we'll be looking out on to a main road . . . at least I hope it will be a main road. And if that comes about the fields at the back will be built on. It'll never be like this. That's what we've got to face up to.'

'I can face up to anything as long as you're there.' They stared at each other, and the time passed and neither of them made a move until Corny, putting his joined hands, which looked like one large fist, between his knees, concentrated his gaze on them as he said, 'There's something I want to say to you. I don't suppose I'll ever mention it again after we're married, and . . . and I find it difficult to say it now. And that's funny because all the time inside it's what I'm feeling. . . . It's just this. I . . . I want to say thanks for having me, Mary Ann.'

'Aw. Aw, Corny.' The sound was like a painful whimper, a surprised whimper.

'I mean it.' He had raised his eyes to her again. 'All the time, inside, I'm grateful. It started a long time ago. I think it was when we walked together through Jarrow for the first time. You remember? And when his lordship' – he motioned his head towards the house on the hill – 'when he stopped the car and ordered you inside and I yelled at him. I remember the very words I used: "Aa'm as good as you lot any day. Aye, Aa am. An' Aa'll show you. By God! Aa will that." That's what I said. . . . Well, I haven't shown him very much, only that I don't look upon him as God Almighty. But it was on that day that I became grateful to you inside, for you didn't want to leave me. And then you asked me to your party and we went walking after and you tried to teach me grammar' – his hand moved slowly up and gripped hers – 'and with your mother and the old fellow openly against me, and your school friends horrified at me accent, me clothes, and me scruffy look, you faced them all and stood up for me. It was that I remembered when I was in America. All the time I kept saying to meself, Who among all those fine pieces—' His mouth again gave a small, wry twist, but there was no laughter on his face as he went on – 'I said to meself, which one of them would have championed me, me as I was as a lad, for what I lacked in looks I didn't make up in charm, and I was too well aware of it. So my weapon was defiance, open defiance. Your da believed in me and that helped, but it was you, Mary Ann, you who brought me up out of the mire.'

'Oh, Corny!' The tears were once again raining down her cheeks. She had no voice with which to protest.

He rose to his feet and drew her gently into his arms, and as he bent his head and buried his face in her hair he muttered, 'So thanks, Mary Ann.'

It was too much, really too much. She wasn't used to people thanking her, and all day everybody had been thanking her: her mother, Mr. Lord, Lettice, and now Corny. And what was more, she hadn't done anything, she hadn't. She knew she hadn't really done anything in her life to help anybody; she just did what she wanted to do, what pleased her. She was selfish she was. Recrimination, self-denigration, was atacking her on all sides when Corny, pushing her from him and gripping her by the shoulders, and in his now recognizable voice hissed down at her, 'But mind, I'm tellin' you, I'm not keeping this up. I've said it and that's the finish, understand?' He shook her gently, and as she laughed through her tears and he pulled her fiercely towards him again the front door bell rang.

As the sound pierced the house it also pierced Mary Ann's memory, and, clapping her hand over her mouth, she whispered between her fingers, 'Me grannie! We forgot about the bus. Oh! Oh, heavens above! Nobody thought to meet the bus.' She scampered from him into the hall, there to meet Lizzie coming out of the kitchen. Pushing her mother back into the room, she gabbled in a whisper, 'It'll be me grannie.'

It was now Lizzie's turn to put her hand to her mouth, and she turned her head over her shoulder and looked towards Mike, saying under her breath, 'I clean forgot. Oh, there'll be murder.'

'Is the room ready?' said Mike, coming forward.

'Oh yes, that's all right. But how could I forget about her coming to stay?'

'Well,' said Mike with a grin, 'that's to be understood; it'll be the first time she'll have slept under our roof.'

As the bell sounded again, a continued ring now, Corny said, 'Will I go and open it?' and Lizzie answered, 'No, no, I'll go and get it over.'

'Now don't tell me that you've been so very busy and occupied that you forgot.' The avalanche hit Lizzie as she opened the door. 'There I was in the dark, out in no-man's-land. You could fall in the ditch and not be found until you're dead. Talk about thoughtlessness!' She was in the hall now and the very hairs of her head seemed to be quivering, and as her hold-all hit the floor it was as if she had thrown it from a great height. 'Froze I am. Talk about a reception. You could be murdered on these roads. An' would that have mattered, says you.'

'Give me your coat, Gran.'

What!' Mrs. McMullen turned on her granddaughter and glared at her; then she put her head on one side as if she hadn't heard aright. And perhaps she hadn't, because never before had she heard Mary Ann speak to her in this gentle, quiet way, nor offer to relieve her of her outdoor things. Her head straight once again, she replied, 'I'm still able to take me own coat off, thank you. And don't come all smarmy with me, for it's past the eleventh hour. It's too late now.'

Mary Ann, her face tight now, left the hall and went into the kitchen, there expecting to have a sympathetic exchange of glances with her da, and Corny. But the room was empty, until Sarah came hobbling from the scullery and towards her, saying softly, 'Corny says to tell you he's going straight back to the house after church, and Mike says to tell you' – her smile broadened here – 'that he and his son are going to the house now. . . . Pronto, and they hope to get the sitting-room done tonight.'

'Oh.' Mary Ann shook her head helplessly. 'Then motioning it backwards, she whispered, 'She's her old self, only worse. It's going to be a lovely evening.'

'We'll go in the front room, there's plenty to do.'

'I'd forgotten clean about her coming.'

'I hadn't,' said Sarah. 'But I didn't think it was so late. Ssh! . . .' She moved forward, hoping to reach a chair before the visitor should enter the room. But this she did not accomplish, and Mrs. McMullen stood surveying her erratic progress with a cold eye in a flaming face; then herself moving towards the fire, she looked at Sarah as she passed her, saying, 'Why don't you use your wheel-chair, girl?'

The question and all it implied caused Sarah's head to droop and the sight of this was too much for Mary Ann. She had prayed last night to Our Lady to give her the strength to be nice to her grannie, at least until the wedding was over, and she had started off well. She had spoken nicely to her and what had she got? Well, if she wanted it that way she could have it, wedding or no wedding. How she spoke to her was one thing, but to tell Sarah that she looked awful when she was walking, and that's what she had meant, was another. Looking boldly now at the bane of her life, she declared, 'Sarah doesn't need a chair, she's walking fine, she's getting better every day. Anyway, who would have thought this time last year that she would have been on her feet at all; and, what's more, driving a car. She. . . .'

'All right, all right, madam. I thought it wouldn't be long before you started. It's well I know you and can't be taken in. Your good intentions are about as strong as a May Day wind. You're still the . . .'

'Are you ready for a cup of tea, Ma?' Lizzie was looking towards the old woman, the tight, defensive look back on her face again, for although this woman was her mother she held thoughts akin to her daughter's concerning her.

'Well, as I haven't broken my fast since dinner-time I suppose I am ready for a cup of tea . . . and a bite of something. But if you're busy, don't stop what you're doing, for of course you must have been very busy to forget that I was coming.'

'I didn't forget you were coming, only I didn't think it was as late as it was.'

'You still have clocks.' The terrible old woman turned her gaze up to the mantelpiece; then she sighed and lay back in the chair. It was as if the first onslaught was over.

Lizzie turned to the table and began preparing her mother a meal, and Sarah, looking towards Mary Ann where she stood in a somewhat undecided manner near the door, said, 'If you'll bring me the box with your veil in, Mary Ann, I'll fix the wreath – it'll save us doing it in the morning – and now that there's nobody in you can try it on.'

'Veil? Wreath? I didn't know you were going to be married in white.'

'You did, Mother.' Lizzie spoke without turning round. 'We told you a while back.'

'You didn't tell me. You talked about it over my head, and as far as I could gather you decided against it. And it would have been wiser if you had stuck to that, for she's not big enough for white. . . . And as for those two sisters of his being bridesmaids. . . . Huh!'

Lizzie signalled across the room to Mary Ann now, warning her with a look not to take any notice, and as she watched her daughter swelling visibly with indignation she put in quickly, 'The girls look bonny enough when they're dressed. As for Mary Ann's frock, it's lovely, and she looks lovely in it.' And on this she nodded to Mary Ann as if to stress the truth of her statement.

'Huh!' Mrs. McMullen looked up at one corner of the ceiling, and then to the other, as if searching for inspiration for her invective; then turning her gaze in the direction of Sarah, she said in a conversational tone, 'White weddings and no honeymoons don't go together. What do you say? You managed a honeymoon, and under the circumstances you should have been the last one to tackle it. . . . You know what I mean?'

Sarah knew what she meant only too well, and in this moment she fully understood Mary Ann's hate of her grannie, for she was a dreadful old woman, cruel.

'We don't want a honeymoon.' Mary Ann's voice, in spite of Lizzie's silent, imploring gaze, came barking across the kitchen now. 'I could have a honeymoon, as you call it, if I'd wanted it, but I don't want to waste money staying in some strange hotel. We'll have a honeymoon all right, but we'll have it in our own home.'

'All right, all right, madam, stop your bawling; I can make a remark, can't I? But no, I should have learned by now I can't open me mouth in this house. My God!' Mrs. McMullen shook her head sadly. 'If you can't act like a human being the night afore your wedding you never will be able to. . . . I hold out no hope for your future happiness if this is how you mean to start off. Anyway, truth to tell, now that we're on, I might as well say that I've never held out much hope for you in that direction, so you have it, not with the partner you've picked. Bairns and a scrubbing brush, that's your future. As I can read anything I can read that.'

'Mother! Now look' – Lizzie was standing above the old lady, her face white and strained, her forefinger wagging violently – 'if you're going to stay the night, and I hope you are, you've got to keep a civil tongue in your head.'

'Me! A civil—'

'You, yes. A civil tongue in your head. There's nobody starts these things only you. Now I'm warning you.'

'Oh, I only needed this ...' Mrs. McMullen closed her eyes. 'That's all I needed, you to start on me. Anyway, I hope I've got it in me to understand, 'cos I saw the minute I entered the door you were all het up. And is it any wonder? If everything I hear is true ... if only half I hear is true, it's understandable that your nerves are all of a frazzle. ... Tell me. Are you still being visited by the Radleys, or are the visits going the other way now? For by what I hear ...'

Mary Ann seemed to shoot across the room to her mother's side, and from there she glared at her grannie and, leaning threateningly towards the old woman, cried at her, 'You know what I wish? You know what I wish?' Her voice dropping suddenly, she added through her clenched teeth, 'I wish you would drop down dead, you old—'

'Mary Ann!' Lizzie, seizing her by the shoulders, pushed her towards the hall, then into the front room, and there she put her arms around her and held her as once more she burst into tears, angry tears now, bitter tears; and looking up at her mother, Mary Ann stammered, 'Oh ... on the night be ... before me wedding she's made me say a thing like th ... that. It was awful, I know, but it's true, Ma, it's true. But f ... fancy me saying it.' She was crying loudly now, and Lizzie hushed her and rocked her as if she was a little girl, the little girl who had many, many times wished her grannie dead. And now Mary Ann, raising her head again, spluttered, 'Scrub ... scrubbing brushes and b ... bairns, that's what she said, that's all Corny can give me, scrubbing brushes and b ... bairns.'

'One scrubbing brush,' said Lizzie with a faint smile.

'What, Ma?' She was sniffing loudly now.

'Bairns, and a scrubbing brush,' Lizzie explained, 'just one scrubbing brush.'

'Oh.' Mary Ann slowly began to glean the funny side of it all, and weakly she returned Lizzie's smile. And Lizzie, stroking her hair back from her wet brow, said softly, 'There's worse things than bairns and a scrubbing brush, if you're happy with the man that provides both.'

CHAPTER TEN

'But, Mrs. McBride, you've got to come to the church; Corny would go mad.'

'Now look, me lass, I proffered to come over here so that I could see to things when you had all gone, and have everything nice and ready when you come back.'

'But everything is ready, and Jonesy and his wife are staying behind, it's all arranged. What's got into you?' Mary Ann's high tone dropped. 'It won't be me wedding if you're not there. And I'm telling you, he'll go mad.'

'Huh! He'll know nothing about it. He'll be so taken up wondering if you're going to come or not. They're all like that at the last minute.'

'But why? It's always been understood you'd be there.'

Fanny turned from Mary Ann and walked down the length of the large barn, and as she walked she moved her head to the right, and the left, looking at the tables set as yet with only crockery and flowers, and, going to the top table, she gazed at the two chairs, bigger than the rest, like two thrones awaiting their occupants. Then turning and facing Mary Ann, who had followed her, she said, on a deep sigh, 'Well, knowing you, you won't stop till you get to the bottom of it, so it's like this, plain and simple, I'm not going to go into the church and disgrace you both in me old togs.'

Mary Ann's mouth opened and shut like that of a dying fish, and then she brought out, 'But, you've got new clothes . . . you were getting new clothes.'

'Aye, so I thought.' Mrs. McBride examined the skin on the back of her large, wrinkled hands. Then she repeated quietly, 'Aye, so I thought, right until just a week ago when it was too late to do anything about it. You see' – she lifted her eyes to Mary Ann – 'our Florrie said she would get me a couple of clubs, enough to get me a coat and hat and be shod decent, and I waited and waited, never thinking but that she would get them for me. And then over she comes at the last minute, on Wednesday night it was, saying she can't get any more, for the whole crowd of them want so much of this and that, and she had gone over her credit, far over. ... Aw, suppose it wasn't too late even then. If I had dropped a word to our Phil he would have been down from Newcastle like a shot and rigged me out – he's wanted to do it time and time again – but as I said, what do I want new clothes for, I'm never out of the door except to go to early mass on a Sunday, and along to the shop. If I got new clothes, I've always said to him, what would I do with them? They'd just hang there and rot.'

'But Corny would have ... he would have seen to everything.'

'I know, lass. Don't I know he would have seen to everything ... and beggared himself still further. I've had to put me foot down afore where that 'un's concerned, and I'm keeping it down from now on that he's a married man, for, refuse how I may, he's left me something every week; come back and pushed it under the door he has after we've gone for each other hell for leather. Oh, I know Corny would have me rigged out like a duchess, but, Mary Ann' – she moved her head slowly – 'I'm an independent spirit, I've never asked anybody for anythin' in me life. Why don't you get supplementary? they say. You've earned it, they say; it isn't charity, it's yours by rights, they say. Huh! ... I know what's mine by rights, so I'm not goin' after any supplementary an' havin' a man comin' to me house checking on what I've got and sayin' to me, "With all those children scattered all over the country you shouldn't be wantin' supplementary, now should you?" Aw, I know. No, Mary Ann, what I can't have I've always made it a point of doin' without. And so there you have it. So you just keep quiet, me dear, and no one will be any the wiser but that I was in church. I can say to them here that I'm comin' in the last car, an' at that time I won't be around.'

'No. No.' Mary Ann shook not only her head but her whole body. 'You're coming, and not in the last car. I tell you Corny'll go mad. And don't think he won't miss you;

he'll be standing in the front of the church and he'll see everybody, and it'll upset him if he doesn't catch sight of you.'

'Nonsense, nonsense. There's only one thing that would
upset him this day and that would be if you didn't arrive.
Why . . . do you think he'll say, "Hold your hand a minute,
hold everything, I must go and find me grannie"?' Fanny let
out a bellow of a laugh at her own joke, and Mary Ann
laughed too. Then stopping abruptly, she said, 'You're
coming, clothes or no clothes,' and, turning from her, she ran
down the barn, out across the sunlit farmyard, up the path
and into the back door, where the buzz of noise came at her
like a blow. The house was full. She had never seen so many
people in it. Sarah met her, saying, 'Where have you been?
Mam's looking all over for you. It's time you were getting
ready.'

'Where's me da?'

'With my dad in the front room, I think. And Corny's
father and the lads are there. . . . What's the matter?'

'I'll tell you in a minute.' Mary Ann made her way
through the kitchen which was packed to capacity. People
were standing, and sitting, and talking, and she heard the
tail end of Mrs. Flanagan's voice saying in high, refined
tones, 'And he thinks the world of her. He must do, mustn't
he, to buy her a car after setting her up in a bungalow.'

Some section of her mind told Mary Ann that Mrs. Flanagan had heard of Mr. Lord's generous wedding present to
herself and Corny and was proving to somebody that it was
nothing compared with what he had given to Sarah. She
could smile at this.

The front room seemed full of men of all ages.

'Da . . . Da.' She tugged at his arm.

'Aren't you away upstairs getting ready?' Mike looked
tenderly down at her, and she answered, 'I want you a
minute.'

As she went into the hall, followed by Mike. Mrs. McMullen came out of the kitchen and made her way to the front
room, remarking in passing, to no one in particular,
'Common as muck, the lot of them.'

Her grannie, Mary Ann knew, was referring to Corny's
mother and father and the squad of children, and although

she would have died rather than agree with anything her grannie said, she did think they could behave a bit better than they did. Corny's father was useless with regards to keeping his tribe in order, and his mother wasn't much better; she just shouted and the lads just laughed at her.

'What is it?' asked Mike.

'Come outside a minute.' She took his hand and drew him through the front door and round the corner of the house. And there she said hastily, 'It's Mrs. McBride. You know what, she's not coming to the wedding because she has no new clothes.'

'Not comin'. . . . No new clothes! But didn't they see to that?'

She told him briefly what had happened, and when she had finished he stood looking down at her with his face screwed up. 'Hell for a tale that,' he said. 'Well, to my mind she must be at your weddin'. What do you think?'

'I think the same, Da. She's always been in my life. . . . I mean she's closer . . . well, than most people. But apart from that, Corny . . . he'll go mad if she's not there. You know, Da' – her voice sank to a whisper and she glanced about her in case any of Corny's family should be within hearing distance – 'Corny doesn't care two hoots for any of them except her. He loves her.'

'Aye, aye, I think you're right. In fact, I know you are. . . . What time is it?' He looked at his watch. 'Ten past eleven. . . . You leave this to me. Where is she?'

'In the barn, Da.' Her eyes were bright as she whispered, 'you'll take her in . . . get her a coat and things?'

'Yes, just that. . . .' Pausing, he patted her playfully on the cheek. 'You knew I would, didn't you?'

'I hoped so, Da. But . . . . you'll be back in time?'

'I'll be back, never fear. You go upstairs and get dressed, that's the main thing. It won't take me two shakes of a lamb's tail to get into me togs, so go on now an' leave it to me.'

'Thanks, Da.' She reached up and kissed him; then added, 'You might have a job getting her to agree.'

'She'll agree . . . go on now.'

She turned from him and ran into the house, and Lizzie,

136

meeting her in the hall, said, 'Where've you been? Look at the time. Go on up, it's time you were starting. . . . Where's your da?'

'Here a minute.' Mary Ann took her mother by the hand and led her upstairs, and briefly she put her in the picture. And Lizzie said, 'Oh dear. But yes, I see she's got to be there, but . . . but will he have time, will he be back in time? He's got to put a new suit on and you know what he's like with a new suit.'

'It'll be all right, Ma.'

'Well I hope so. . . . Come on, off with your things and let's get started.'

As Mary Ann went to pull her jumper over her head there came a tap on the door, and when Lizzie, her tongue clicking impatiently, opened it, she gave a cry of surprise that turned Mary Ann about, and, her arms still in her jumper, she, too, exclaimed aloud, for there stood Sarah; at one side of her was her father, at the other, Mr. Boyle.

'She's made it,' said Mr. Flanagan proudly. 'We wanted to carry her up, but no. "One at a time," she said, and she's made all sixteen of them.'

Sarah, her face flushed to a deep pink with the exertion of her effort and the triumph over herself, shambled into the room and, flopping into the chair, looked at Mary Ann and laughed as she said, 'I always intended to do it . . . to help you dress like you did me.'

'Aw, Sarah.' Mary Ann put her hand gently on Sarah's head, and as she did so Lizzie exclaimed, 'Well now, well now, we want to get started.' This remark was directed towards the men, and as she was about to close the door on them Mr. Boyle turned a red-faced grin on her, and under his breath he said, 'No disrespect, Lizzie, but—' He paused here and his eyes flashed to Mr. Flanagan, then to Mary Ann, who had turned towards him, then back to Lizzie before he added, 'Has anybody thought of shooting your mother?'

Lizzie forcibly prevented herself from laughing, but from Mary Ann there came a high, gleeful sound and she cried in no small voice, 'Oh, I have, Mr. Boyle.' She had always addressed him as Mr. Boyle and couldn't see herself ever calling him anything else. She had never liked him; in fact if she had asked herself the question she would have answered that she disliked him, but now in a flash she saw him in a different light. He might booze, swear, and not bring his money home, but there, beneath the skin, she saw Corny.

Lizzie prevented him from taking a step into the room as Mary Ann cried, 'We'll get together later and fix up something, eh?'

'Right. Right, Mary Ann, that's a deal.'

'And count me in.' It was little Mr. Flanagan now piping up his face alight with merriment.

Lizzie slammed the door on the two men and, turning to the laughing girls, she said indignantly, 'Really! Really!' But in spite of the reprimand, Mary Ann saw that her mother had her work cut out to stop herself laughing aloud.

'And you!' said Lizzie. 'Standing there with no jumper on.'

'Eeh!' Mary Ann looked down at herself. 'So I was. What are things coming to?' The two girls giggled. Then Mary Ann, about to divest herself further, turned to Lizzie and exclaimed, 'Queenie and Nancy. Who's seeing to them?'

'Their mother. She'll put them right.'

'But will she?' Mary Ann's eyebrows moved up. 'If she sees to them as she does every day I'm going to have two beautiful bridesmaids.'

'She can do things all right when she puts her mind to it, and I've seen them and they're very sweet. Now don't bother about them; get your things off and let's get started.'

As Lizzie moved towards the wardrobe she had to pass the window, and Mary Ann's bedroom window overlooked the farmyard. Lizzie looked at the farmyard so many times a day that now she didn't see it, and she had glanced through the window and reached the wardrobe before she dived back to the window again and there a long-drawn-out 'Ooh!' escaped her.

'What is it?' asked Mary Ann and Sarah together.

'The boys, they're on the silage in their new clothes and their father and your grannie are going at it.'

Mary Ann came to the window and looked down on Corny's two youngest brothers, the nine-year-old twins, who had evidently been enjoying themselves. The silage was kept in a yard apart from the main one, and the boys with long pronged forks in their hands stood now in the opening between the two yards, and even from this distance she could see that their boots were filthy and their clothes bespattered. They had only once before been at the farm and everybody remembered their visit. The open spaces seemed to have a maddening effect on them, for they had raced like wild horses from one place to the other. She brought her eyes from them to their father. She could see that he was smiling, but she could also see that he was wagging a large forefinger in her grannie's face and the forefinger, denying the smile, spelled out to Mary Ann, 'Now look here, old lady, you mind your business and I'll mind mine.'

As Lizzie opened the window and called down to her mother, Mrs. McMullen's voice came high and clear on the crisp, sun-filled air, saying, 'Disgrace, that's what they are; like young pigs on the wrong side of the fence.'

'Oh, look!' As the exclamation was drawn from Mary Ann she pulled her mother back from the window and whispered urgently, 'Mr. Lord, Tony and Lettice . . . coming down the hill.'

'Oh no!' Lizzie lifted her hand to her head. 'They'll run into that, and if my mother corners Mr. Lord. . . . Oh, why isn't Mike here! And where's Michael in all this?' She turned and looked at Sarah as if she were responsible for Michael's non-appearance in the yard. Then Mary Ann put in, 'Look, Ma, you go on down, I'll manage. And I've got Sarah. Go on, see to things. Don't let me grannie meet him, not out there. And if he sees the twins like that, he'll be so wild, and . . . and it'll look bad for Corny. Oh go on, Ma.'

'Aw. Dear, dear.' Lizzie hesitated only for a moment then hurried from the room, and Mary Ann and Sarah looked at each other. Then Mary Ann, going to her dressing-table, sat down and through the mirror said to Sarah, 'Me wedding day. I just can't believe it's me wedding day.' She gave a wry smile. 'All these little things happening, just like any other day, or more so, and yet I don't feel the same as on other days. I've . . . I've got a racing feeling inside. . . . You know what I mean?'

Sarah nodded through the mirror.

'I don't know whether I want to race to the church or race away from it.' They both giggled at this, then Mary Ann went on, but seriously now, 'For a while last night I felt wonderful, not a bit afraid or anything. When we stood outside, just before he went, and the moon was shining and everything was so quiet, it was then I felt wonderful, happier than I'd ever been in my life. I had a sort of safe feeling with it. I felt as long as I was with Corny everything would always be all right. . . . You know?'

Again Sarah nodded through the mirror. 'Yes, I know. And it's the right feeling. If you feel like that nothing much can touch you.'

'You think so?'

'I know so.'

Mary Ann, staring hard at Sarah now, saw that she was looking at a woman, that Sarah had grown up, leaving her still a child. She said thoughtfully, 'But the feeling didn't stay, for as soon as I woke this morning I felt frightened, in fact I wished it wasn't going to happen, and I wanted to be some place quiet and think and try to get a nice feeling inside.' She spread out her hands. 'But look at it. Everything's happened that could. And people coming far too early; his mother was to bring the girls at half-past ten and what did she do but bring the whole bang lot of them with her . . . and at ten o'clock. Of course there was one person delighted . . . me grannie, for she was running out of targets.'

As if in answer to this jibe Mrs. McMullen's voice came penetratingly through the floor, and Mary Ann put her hands over her ears and, swinging round and facing Sarah, her eyes dancing, whispered, 'What do you bet, when Father Owen says 'If anyone knows of any impediment, etc.,' she doesn't get to her feet and shout, "Any impediment! I can give you a round dozen. . . . Now you just listen to me".' Mary Ann had mimicked her grannie's voice, and now the two girls, hands clasped, threw back their heads and laughed, high, gleeful laughter. But in Mary Ann's case it spoke plainly of nervous strain and tension.

It was here, this was the moment. This was the joyous

moment. . . . At least, it should have been joyous but she still felt frightened. She was too young to be married. She should never have said she would do it. Her legs would give way when she was walking down the aisle. And all those people behind her outside the church door, how had they known? Mrs. McBride. Yes, Mrs. McBride. They couldn't get the car near the kerb, and the voices from all over the crowd shouting, 'Eeh! Look, Mary Ann. Hello, Mary Ann. Mary Ann. Oo! Oo!' She had kept her head down but had lifted it to look at a woman as she entered the church door, for the woman had said, and somewhat sadly, 'Aw, hinny, you won't be Mary Ann Shaughnessy for much longer now.'

And she wouldn't be Mary Ann Shaughnessy for much longer. She hadn't thought about that before, she was going to lose her name. She liked her name. MARY ANN SHAUGHNESSY. In a short while she would be Mary Ann Boyle. It sounded awful . . . Mary Ann Boyle. Oh no, she didn't want to be Mary Ann Boyle.

'Are you all right?' Mike was looking down at her, gently drawing her hand through his arm. She looked up at him blinking. She was hot and sweating; her make-up must look awful, and she wanted to cry. . . . Don't be so silly. She blinked rapidly and saw Mike's face, then all of him. He looked grand, did her da. His new suit fitted him to a 'T'. They stared at each other oblivious for the moment of the bustle about them. Somebody was whispering to the brides-maids, 'Hold them like this, don't let them droop.' That would be the posies. The organ was rumbling overhead, waiting for the signal, and in this moment there came to Mary Ann the strange idea that she was inside her da, right inside of him, thinking his thoughts, feeling his feelings, and he, too, wanted to cry. She turned her eyes from him. It was awful, awful. She was going to be married, she should be joyful. What was the matter with her, anyway? MARY ANN BOYLE. Oh, she didn't like that name. She would never be Mary Ann Boyle whatever happened, she wouldn't. Inside herself she would always be Mary Ann Shaughnessy. She would remain Mary Ann Shaughnessy for ever. She wanted to tell her da that she would never be anybody but Mary Ann Shaughnessy. She would always keep his name.

But ... but what was she talking about, for Shaughnessy wasn't his name, not really. ... Anyway, what was in a name?

Mike squeezed her hand and, bending his head sideways down to her, whispered, 'You'll be all right. Don't worry. Do you know something?' He waited.

'What, Da?' Her lips were trembling and she spoke without turning her head.

'You look very beautiful.'

'Oh, Da.' She pressed his arm to her.

'And ... and I'll love you till the day I die. Never forget that.'

Ooh! Oh, he shouldn't have said that, he shouldn't, it was too much. She would burst, she would cry.

There was a movement in front of them; someone said, 'Ready?'

There was bustle behind; a second later the organ swelled into loud chords and she was walking forward out of the dim vestibule, round by the holy water font, in which she had dipped her fingers from the time she could reach it, to the top of the central aisle. The wish was strong in her now that they could go down the side aisle and that she could be married at the altar of the Holy Family, for they had always been part of her family. ... Where had all the people come from? The church was almost full. Her high-heeled shoes slipped just the tiniest bit on the grating and she felt the heat from the pipes coming up under her dress. She had loved to stand over the grating in the cold weather and get her legs warm. Sometimes the boiler went wrong and the church was as cold as death, but today the boiler was all right, Father Owen had seen to that. The church was warm, the atmosphere was warm, the people's faces, those turned towards her, were warm. She didn't look at them but she could feel their warmth. But when she approached her own people she looked at them. Her mother, oh, her mother looked bonny, lovely, young, even though her eyes were sad; and there was Sarah, bright-faced, happy-looking Sarah; and Lettice and Tony. Tony was looking full at her and she exchanged a direct glance with him, which said something, which meant something, but which in this moment she couldn't decipher.

142

Then there was Mrs. Flanagan, proud, pinched-faced, but smiling Mrs. Flanagan, kind at last; and now the face of her grannie. . . . Oh! Why had she to look at her grannie, why at this moment had she to look at her grannie, for belated maternal love and benevolence had not touched her grannie's countenance. It was the same as she had always seen it. But there was another face, a face really showing love and benevolence . . . and pride: the face of Mr. Lord. His eyes were on her, pale-blue misty eyes, but piercing into her, sending her a message, and she answered it, sending him her love and gratitude for as long as he might need it.

Then on the other side of the aisle were Corny's people. His mother and father, their faces full of smiling good-will. . . . Why had she never liked them? – because they were really likeable. What did it matter if she didn't keep her house clean? And there was all Corny's relations filling three pews . . . Corny had said they would fill three pews. But in the very first seat of the first pew was a face whose beam spread itself over all of them. It was topped by a blue velour hat of unspotted newness, it was the wrinkled, battered face, the wise face of her friend, Fanny McBride, and the knowledgeable eyes held Mary Ann's for more than a second until they seemed to usher her gaze to the front, to where, on the altar steps, stood Father Owen, kind, loving, understanding Father Owen. . . . They had said to her, 'Why do you want to be married in Jarrow Church? You're nearer to Pelaw.' But Jarrow had always been her church, and Father Owen was her priest. Father Owen knew all about her, everything, the good and the bad. Now Father Owen's gaze drew her eyes with his and they travelled past their Michael, tall and handsome, a young edition of her father, to someone else, tall . . . and handsome. For Corny in this moment looked handsome to her. His red hair was lying for once in well-brushed order, his deep-set dark eyes were warm and shining, his wide-lipped mouth was gentle. She wished he wasn't so tall, she wished she wasn't so small, she wished . . . she wished. . .

'MARY ANN . . . MARY ANN.'

It was as if he was calling her name.

'MARY ANN, OH, MARY ANN.'

143

Mike let her go. She felt the moment of release as if he had thrust her from him. She was by herself, getting nearer to Corny. She was close to him now, and as she looked at him for a moment his eyes blotted out everything about her. Gently their message sank into her and she felt it lift her round to face the priest.

GOOD-BYE, MARY ANN SHAUGHNESSY.

Good-bye, Mary Ann Shaughnessy.

Good-bye, Mary Ann.

Good-bye.

Good-bye.

'Wilt thou take this woman . . .?'